"Talking to yourself?" The inquiry was sarcastic

Frankie turned around, color staining her cheeks.

"I was talking to the donkeys." It was difficult to meet Mike's eyes, but from his cool-as-a-cucumber manner, Frankie thought indignantly, last night might never have happened. She was filled with acute embarrassment, vividly remembering that kiss. A kiss he'd intended as punishment—but which had nearly become something else for her, something far more disturbing.

"And what are you doing here?" she snapped. "I'm surprised you have the nerve to come after last night."

"Last night?" He sounded puzzled. Then his brows rose quizzically. "Oh, that. Don't worry, Frankie, it's not something I intend to repeat. I didn't derive any satisfaction from it—any more than you did."

Annabel Murray has pursued many hobbies. She helped found an arts group in Liverpool, England, where she lives with her husband and two daughters. She loves drama: she appeared in many stage productions and went on to write an award-winning historical play. She uses all her experiences—holidays being no exception—to flesh out her characters' backgrounds and create believable settings for her romance novels.

IMPOSSIBLE INHERITANCE

Annabel Murray

Harlequin Books

TORONTO • NEW YORK • LONDON
AMSTERDAM • PARIS • SYDNEY • HAMBURG
STOCKHOLM • ATHENS • TOKYO • MILAN

Original hardcover edition published in 1991
by Mills & Boon Limited

ISBN 0-373-17098-X

Harlequin Romance first edition November 1991

For Tom: who always believes in me.

IMPOSSIBLE INHERITANCE

CHAPTER ONE

'DAMMIT! Oh, dammit!'

Glaring at it as if it were the instrument's fault, Frankie Latimer slammed the telephone receiver back to its rest on the bureau. She had counted on Nigel being in. Her fiancé usually was at home on Saturday afternoons and she was dying to share her news with him—the news of her unexpected legacy. Perhaps now, at long last, they would be able to get married.

'*Please* tell Nigel I rang,' she had begged his mother, 'as soon as he gets in. It's very important.' But she wondered if Mrs Greaves *would* tell him. So often in the past messages had gone undelivered.

Frankie was well aware that Mrs Greaves did not approve of her as a wife for her only son. But it was a disapproval the older woman had been careful—and cunning enough—to hide from Nigel, so that he always looked mystified when Frankie hinted at her belief that his mother did not like her. And Frankie could not do more than hint. Nigel was an affectionate and loyal son, genuinely blind, Frankie believed, to his mother's true character.

And, after all, it was these qualities of loyalty and affection that had first drawn Frankie to him—long before she had even met his mother.

Someone—she could not remember who—had once

told her, 'Look at the way a man treats his mother if you want to know how he'll treat his wife.'

Frankie often wondered if *her* mother had ever taken an opportunity to observe how her husband had treated Granny Latimer. If so, she had not profited by the experience. And Frankie was determined that *her* marriage should not repeat the mistakes of her mother's. *Her* husband was going to be reliable, hard-working, a rock-steady support—all the things Bob Latimer had *not* been.

His working life had been spasmodic, interspersed by long periods of so-called 'back trouble'—an ailment that had been hard to prove but equally impossible to *dis*-prove. At such times his wife, Lily, had been the sole breadwinner. And when he *was* working and 'in funds', Bob Latimer had frequented public houses. He had also been an inveterate gambler and a reckless squanderer.

It was sad, Frankie thought, and not for the first time, when you had no loving memories of a parent, only anger at the way they had treated their partner.

These thoughts brought Frankie back to the subject of her legacy. Aunt Francesca, her mother's somewhat eccentric great-aunt, had never approved of Bob Latimer and had always been frank in her opinion of him.

And one day Aunt Francesca had gone too far. 'He's got back trouble all right, Lily—he's *spineless*! I was going to remember you in my will but there's no way I intend to have that great layabout profit by it. And I know you, any money you've ever had has always found its way into his pockets.'

But, like her daughter, Lily had set great value on

loyalty. Her husband might not be loyal but in her eyes that did not exempt *her*, and from that day an irreparable rift had divided Lily Latimer and her great-aunt. Which had been a pity, not only for a lonely old lady but also for Frankie, who had been named for her.

Still seated near the telephone, in case Nigel should call back, Frankie had been rifling through the bureau's cluttered pigeon-holes and now she found what she sought, a folder containing a bundle of faded photographs. Following the disagreement with her great-aunt, Lily Latimer had ripped these from her albums and consigned them to the wastepaper basket. But Frankie had surreptitiously rescued them.

As a child and as the teenager she was then, Frankie had adored her great-great-aunt. Looking back, she knew Francesca had felt the same way about her. Her eyes misted over as she pored over the snapshots, many of them taken during holidays she had spent with the old lady. One of them, her favourite, showed 'the two Frankies', as it was labelled, outside a picturesque Kentish cottage and included some of the animals of which old Francesca had always been fond. A cat, two lop-eared dogs of uncertain breed and in the distance a gaggle of geese—creatures which Frankie had always secretly feared.

How she had looked forward to and enjoyed those holidays, which, she realised now, had mostly coincided with bad patches in her parents' life.

'I'm sorry we lost touch, Auntie,' Frankie murmured now, quite unaware that she spoke aloud. 'But Mum didn't want me to see you and I couldn't go against her whilst she was alive. And since she died last year—

well, somehow there's never been time. But I'd rather have had you alive than have the legacy. Truly I would.'

More than ever, Frankie wished Nigel had been available to talk to—not just about her inheritance but about her aunt. There were so many memories flooding back now and no one with whom to share them.

Saturday teatime came and went but still Nigel had not telephoned. Frankie wondered again where he could be. With any other man of her acquaintance she could have made a shrewd guess—it was the middle of the football season. But Nigel did not follow any kind of sport. Outside of his work, most of his interests were home-based. A DIY fanatic, he had made his mother's home and garden a veritable showpiece. In fact Frankie had first met Nigel in the local hardware store, where she had been purchasing some new dust-bags for her mother's vacumn cleaner.

At least when they were married, Frankie thought, she would see something of him. He would not be forever at the pub—as her father had been—or on the golf course, like the husbands of some of her friends.

At last Frankie could wait no longer. Mrs Greaves had probably forgotten again, deliberately or not, to give Nigel the message. She dialled the familiar number once more.

'He's *still* not in?' she said in dismayed disbelief. But she did not like to accuse Mrs Greaves of fibbing and, besides, the older woman would be unlikely to lie when her son was within earshot. 'He hasn't been back at all? Do you know where he is? Perhaps I could contact him there?'

But Mrs Greaves did not know. Or did she? Frankie suspected the woman was just being awkward again. A son as considerate as Nigel would not leave his mother without any idea of where to contact him in case of an emergency. Frankie could only repeat her earlier message, that it was important Nigel should get in touch as soon as possible.

She telephoned again on Sunday afternoon. No use trying in the morning. Nigel always escorted his mother to church then.

This time it was Nigel who answered. Frankie could hear the noise of the television in the background. Mrs Greaves always watched the afternoon film.

'Message?' he said when Frankie told him she had spoken twice to his mother the previous day. 'No, I'm afraid not, or I would have rung.' And then, lowering his voice, 'The poor darling is a bit forgetful sometimes. But I don't like to say anything. It upsets and worries her.'

Then why the hell doesn't she write messages down? Frankie thought savagely. Not that she believed for a moment in Mrs Greaves's failing memory.

'So what did you want to talk about?' Nigel asked. But just then, as Frankie began to speak, the noise-level of the television rose to deafening proportions. Frankie could just picture Mrs Greaves pressing the volume button on the remote control and tut-tutting as she always did if anyone spoke above a whisper. That, and her habit of flicking restlessly from station to station, had nearly driven Frankie insane on the occasions when she had shared mother's and son's viewing.

'Sorry,' Nigel apologised. 'I didn't catch what you said. Mum's watching one of her favourite films and her hearing isn't what it used to be.'

Frankie repressed a cynical laugh. She happened to know that his mother's hearing was particularly acute, especially when it came to overhearing things not meant for her ears.

'What did you want me for?' Nigel repeated.

'I think we'd better leave it till this evening,' Frankie said and had to repeat her words to compete with the blaring television. 'I suppose you *are* still coming tonight?' she almost shouted.

She was seething as she hung up. The old bat! When you had been bubbling over for the past forty-eight hours, wanting to share your news—and your emotions—with the man in your life, to be frustrated by his contrary mother and her sickly golden oldies. . .

Nigel was on time that evening, another of his reliable traits. Frankie had taken her usual care in preparing for their evening together. Her long red hair was newly washed and brushed, her tall, slender figure—a decided asset to her modest but steadily improving career as a photographic model—was alluringly clad in misty green wool which made her eyes an even darker green by comparison.

The expression in Nigel's eyes and his enthusiastic greeting were a satisfactory tribute to the result of her efforts.

'Now, then, what were all the phone calls in aid of?' he asked as they sat down to eat.

Frankie had gone to a great deal of trouble too over the meal. Nigel had very conservative tastes where food was concerned. His idea was a traditional meat and two veg, followed by a solid pudding with custard. 'Just like Mother makes,' he would always say with satisfaction.

'Do you remember me telling you about my mother's great-aunt?' Frankie asked. 'The one I was named for? Who disapproved of Mum marrying Dad?'

'Popped her clogs, has she?' Nigel guessed cheerfully, with his mouth full.

Frankie frowned a little but made no comment. After all, she could hardly expect Nigel to share her grief for an elderly woman he had never met.

'She's dead, yes. She was incredibly ancient, of course. She must have been quite old even when I was a child.'

'Has she left you something, then? Is that what all the excitement was about?' And, as Frankie nodded, 'Well, how about that? I didn't know I was courting an heiress.' He reached across the table and patted her hand. 'You're not eating,' he urged her.

'*I* didn't know I stood to inherit anything—until yesterday. It's not often there's anything interesting in Saturday's post. But it's made me feel rather sad. I was very fond of her, you know. I——'

'How much has the old girl left you?' Nigel enquired, busily polishing his plate with a crust of bread. Nothing ever seemed to disturb *his* appetite.

'Goodness, I don't know yet. The letter was just the

usual solicitor's jargon. "Something to your advantage—call upon us at your earliest convenience."'

'Did you know she had money?'

'Not really. But I don't think kids bother about that sort of thing. At least I didn't.'

'Perhaps it won't *be* money,' Nigel suggested. 'Perhaps it'll be some old trinket—a locket, with a curl of her dead lover's hair.'

Frankie smiled wryly. 'Aunt Francesca didn't have a lover as far as I know. She didn't seem to think much of men.'

'A blighted love-affair?'

'I don't know. But anyway, I don't think a solicitor would say "to your advantage" if it wasn't something worth having. Nigel, if it *is* money, it might mean we can get married *this* year, instead of next.'

'When will you find out?'

'Tomorrow afternoon. I rang the solicitors as soon as I'd read the letter. Luckily someone was working Saturday morning.'

'Blast!' Nigel exclaimed. 'I won't be around to hear the glad tidings. I've got to go back to Glasgow in the morning. That's where I was yesterday. But of course Mum told you that.'

'She didn't actually,' Frankie said, and—before he could offer the predictable excuse—'You could always phone me tomorrow night?'

'I will if I can. But you know what these business "do"s are like. Sometimes it's difficult to get away until the small hours.

*   *   *

As a rule, Frankie enjoyed her work, a new career which had only taken off in the last year, but already she was beginning to make a name for herself, modelling for an increasing range of products from shampoo right down to footwear.

But that Monday morning her mind was not totally on the job. Once or twice the photographer had to speak sharply to her when a change of pose was required. Nor could she face lunch, her stomach churning with a mixture of excitement and apprehension.

It wasn't just good news she was going to receive but details, perhaps harrowing, of her aunt's final illness and death.

Nerves made her twenty minutes early for her appointment at the solicitors' in the heart of the City, and she had to pace up and down for a while before entering the premises. Aunt Francesca had had a long life, Frankie kept telling herself, and if she hadn't wanted her namesake to enjoy—whatever it was—she would not have left it to her.

The solicitor was just like the solicitor in plays, and several times during his introductory remarks Frankie had to suppress a nervous giggle. Her quirky sense of humour was often her downfall. Sometimes, when posing for the most serious of products, she would see a ridiculous side to it and—as an actress friend of hers once described it—she would corpse.

But when she left the City office, Frankie no longer felt like laughing. For once she could not see the funny side of something. So much for the wedding plans she had been busily making ever since she had received the solicitor's letter. Aunt Francesca's legacy would be no help at all with that, unless of course there was anything worth selling. Not only that, the old lady had appointed a *trustee*, who, the solicitor had said, would furnish Frankie with further details. Worst of all, whatever would Nigel say about her impossible inheritance?

Two days later, on the Wednesday, as Frankie drove out of a still-sleeping Potters Bar, she had yet to learn Nigel's reactions. He was still in Glasgow. And, uncharacteristically for Nigel-the-conscientious, he had not called. And his mother could not—or more likely would not—give Frankie any idea of where to contact him.

Her second-hand red sports car, bought for zipping about town and along motorways, made heavy weather of the rutted country lanes. Ten years ago, she had discovered, old Francesca had sold the Kentish cottage. The place she had called home since then lay just beyond the small remote Cotswold village of Lionswick.

It was still early when Frankie drove through the village, and puddles from an overnight rain splattered the car's bright paintwork and dirtied its windows.

The driveway up to the old farmhouse didn't look much better, she thought as she clattered over a cattle grid. Against its winter backdrop of bare trees and grey skies, the house itself looked not only forbidding but decidedly dilapidated. Probably very little had been spent on its maintenance. Still, at least it *was* a house. It would not have surprised Frankie to find that her eccentric relative had lived in a caravan.

The key she had been given obviously fitted the front

door but all Frankie's attempts to open it failed. Either it had not been used in years or the door was bolted on the inside. She went round to the back, noting grimly that the garden—like the house—had been sacrificed to her aunt's prevailing obsession.

A battered and muddy Land Rover was parked by the back door, which, despite the January weather, stood wide open.

Frankie's heart beat a little faster. She had not expected to encounter squatters and she regretted her impulsive decision not to wait until Nigel could accompany her.

Whoever was in the kitchen was behaving as though quite at home. A radio was blaring out the latest pop record to the accompaniment of rattling utensils and there was an all-pervading smell of. . . Ugh! Frankie wrinkled her shapely nose. She could not find an adequate description.

Nervous she might be, but Frankie was not without courage. She marched across the threshold.

'Who are *you*?' she demanded imperiously of the broad, check-shirted back. 'And what the hell are you doing in my house?'

He turned away from the stove and the large galvanised buckets which were responsible for the unpleasant emissions. He was big and broad, black-haired, swarthy-complexioned—and ugly, was Frankie's first assessment, an opinion she was later to revise.

'*Your* house?' He moved towards her.

Frankie was tall herself. But this man towered over her and she was hard put to it to stand her ground as dark grey eyes looked her up and down in what she considered to be an odiously insolent fashion. Not at all the way men usually looked at her.

For Frankie had a very special presence. Along with her willowy figure, long dancer's legs and full breasts, she had also been blessed with great facial beauty. She had striking green eyes, vibrant auburn hair and a straight, almost Grecian nose set between cheekbones both high and slanted.

Yes, Frankie was accustomed to strong male reaction to her appearance, and blatant sexual appraisal she could cope with, treat as it deserved. But this was something quite different.

'*My* house!' she repeated firmly, standing her ground.

'I suppose that means you're "Francesca the Second"? Frankie Latimer?' To Frankie's incredulous ears he actually sounded disapproving. What right did *he* have to disapprove of *her*? He was the intruder.

'Yes, I'm Frankie Latimer. Who are *you*?' she repeated. 'And what *do* you think you're doing?' She looked pointedly towards the stove, at the same time making a little moue of disgust.

'The name's Mike.' He did not offer to shake hands. Just as well, Frankie thought distastefully, seeing that his hands—large and strong-looking in proportion with the rest of him—were liberally daubed with whatever was in the buckets.

He had a deep voice which seemed to come from somewhere way down in the broad chest and which would have been pleasant if it had been friendly. He rubbed the palms of his hands over his faded jeans.

'As to what I'm doing—well—until you move in and

take over, someone has to feed the donkeys.' Icy fingers skittered down her spine as again there was that comprehensive assessment of her face and slim figure, a sardonic eye taking in the smartly tailored outfit, the sheer nylons, the high heels. 'Though I must say you don't look very well equipped to run a donkey sanctuary. You look more like a fashion model.'

'Close,' she told him drily. 'But since I'm not going to——'

'Oh, I *know* what you *are*,' he went on before she could say any more. 'I know *all about you*.' It did not sound as if the knowledge gave him any pleasure. In fact once more he sounded distinctly disapproving, and Frankie's hackles rose still further at this additional evidence of his inexplicable hostility. She wished again that Nigel were with her. He would not have allowed this. . .this roughneck to speak to her that way.

'In that case,' she said stiffly, 'you have the advantage of me, Mr. . .?' She absolutely refused to call him 'Mike'. '*I've* never heard of *you*.'

'How could you,' he retorted swiftly, and now the dark grey eyes were hard, aggressive, 'since you never communicated with your aunt? It seems to me you might have made an effort to visit the old girl occasionally. She had very fond memories of you.'

Frankie gasped. The infernal nerve of the man! Her auburn hair rippled in fiery waves as she tossed her head in rejection of his unfair attack. 'I had my reasons for not visiting,' she told him tartly, 'reasons I don't propose to give you, since they're none of your business.' Then, on a different note, unable to repress her curiosity about this man, 'It sounds as though you knew my aunt rather well?'

'I did.' He lifted the buckets from the stove and set them down on the flagged floor. 'There weren't many days when I hadn't to call in. Donkeys—especially rescued ones—need an awful lot of veterinary care.'

'So you're a vet?' she said with an air of discovery. His strong muscular build and weathered complexion had made her wonder if he was a local farmer.

'Ten out of ten!' His tone was one of sarcastic congratulation. 'As bright as you're beautiful.' But it did not sound like a compliment. Again he looked her up and down, a process Frankie was beginning to find increasingly annoying and—yes—disturbing. His gaze was too penetrating. He was large and aggressively masculine—not as ugly as she had first thought—and despite his self-introduction he was a complete stranger. 'Now, I don't suppose you'd care to help me carry these out to the stables?' He indicated the still-steaming buckets.

'Too right I wouldn't!' Frankie said emphatically. 'Even if I could lift one, which I doubt, I've no intention of messing up these clothes.'

His dark eyes were considering. 'If you take off the jacket of that snazzy outfit, there's an old overall of your aunt's hanging behind the door, and some wellingtons in the porch. You look about the same build— even though you're curvaceous where she was angular. They should fit.'

Blushing furiously at the personal remark, Frankie protested. 'Look, Mr. . .whatever your name is, I——'

He ignored the protest. 'You may as well get used to the job. Since all this,' he made an expansive gesture, 'is yours now.'

'You must be mad,' Frankie told him incredulously, 'if you think I have any intention of running this place. I was appalled when the solicitor told me. I can't imagine what Aunt Francesca was thinking of.'

'I can. She was thinking of a tomboyish girl she used to know, who loved the country and animals.' He sounded fierce and once again he looked her over, but this time as though he were trying to visualise that small girl and signally failing. 'She once thought you loved *her* too.'

Frankie met the cold lance of his scrutiny, 'I *did* love Aunt Francesca!' she began, then bit her lip. She didn't *have* to excuse herself to this man.

'Funny way of showing it.'

'Mr. . . Oh, what *is* your name? I——'

'You may as well call me Mike. Your aunt and I never stood on ceremony. And since we'll be seeing a lot of each other——' He didn't sound as if the prospect gave him any pleasure.

'No, we won't,' Frankie interrupted. 'This is not only my first visit but hopefully my last.'

'What does that mean exactly?' There was an angry, suspicious edge to his voice now.

'It means I intend to sell this place. There's no way I——'

'I'd advise you to think again. You see——'

'No need. My mind was made up long before I got here. And now I've seen this. . .' Her full bottom lip curled as she indicated the kitchen, the state of which would have given a Public Health Inspector nightmares.

'I agree it's not a pretty sight. But your aunt was old. She had no one to help her. Looking after the donkeys used up all her time and energy. But for someone young and fit like you. . . And it certainly wouldn't hurt *you* to use a bit of elbow grease.' To her indignation he reached out and grabbed one of her hands and ran a large callused finger over the soft skin and the long, highly polished nails. He spoke scornfully. 'I bet these hands have never been in anything harsher than hand cream.'

'How dare you?' It was not just his presumption, nor his scornful words that made Frankie's voice shake. It was also the very odd feeling that had zipped through her when that rough, work-hardened flesh brushed against hers, a feeling that had not been revulsion, but a wave of excitement so intense that she snatched her hand away and rubbed it against her skirt, not with any intention to insult but to rid herself of those tiny electric shocks. 'Will you get it into your head? I am not——'

'I haven't time to stand here arguing,' Mike interrupted. 'Before you make any more rash decisions, I suggest you come and meet the donkeys.' He strode towards the door, two heavy steaming pails carried in each large hand as easily as if they were a child's plastic buckets.

Frankie had no desire to meet the donkeys but, because there were still a few things she wanted to say to this aggravating man, she followed him. Infuriatingly, he seemed to have taken it for granted she would, because he put down his burden long enough to toss her the overall and waited while she donned the wellingtons. How she would love to shatter that arrogant, self-confident manner of his.

'That's better,' he observed, as she belted the overall about her slim waist. 'It may not be as glamorous, but at least you look more in keeping with the place.'

'Believe me,' she told him with some asperity, 'if it weren't that I've no intention of ruining my clothes or my shoes——'

'Yes,' his voice had that scornful note again, 'those things *would* be more important to someone like you.'

'Someone like me?' she asked suspiciously, but already knowing that the answer would not be a flattering one.

The broad shoulders shrugged. 'A city butterfly—flighty, concerned only with your own appearance. With more interest in selling your beautiful face and body to glossy magazines than in visiting an old woman who loved and missed you.'

'Are those Aunt Francesca's words or yours?' Frankie enquired with dangerous quietness. Her temper was being ridden on a short rein and she was feeling a growing urge to slap him, hard, to leave the mark of her hand across a rugged cheek.

'Mine,' he confirmed. 'But I formed my opinions from what she told me about you, about your career, and from your neglect of her. And I've seen and heard nothing yet to make me change my views. Attractive, highly polished, totally impractical and shallow. *That* about sums you up.'

For a moment Frankie stood stock-still, speechless

with anger. Then, stumbling a little in the too-large
boots, she caught up with him again.

'You are quite the rudest, most insufferable man I've
ever met,' she told him. '*And* you couldn't be more
wrong about me.'

'You could always try and prove it to me,' he
challenged. 'And for a start, get your beautiful hands
dirty. Help me feed the donkeys.'

There were perhaps fifteen or twenty of them, of all
sizes and colours, housed in a range of ancient buildings
around the original farmyard. Frankie was not surprised to discover that the animals' accommodation was
decidedly superior to the house.

Mike began to dole out the warm bran mash. And
somehow a still-seething Frankie found herself helping.

'Not too much for each one,' he warned her. 'Too
much and they'll get colic. This is just a supplementary
diet.'

As they went from animal to animal, Mike told her
each one's name and its history. Some of it made
appalling hearing. Though there was no room for them
in her life these days, Frankie did genuinely like
animals, and several times she felt tears pricking her
eyes. Stories of ill-treatment, malnutrition, some cases
just the result of ignorance. But some were of downright vicious cruelty.

'You're not entirely without a heart, then,' Mike
observed as, after one particularly harrowing tale,
Frankie had to sniff and brush a hand across her eyes.
He sounded a little smug and Frankie was immediately

suspicious. If he thought his sob-stories were going to change her mind. . .

'It's the smell of this bran,' she lied, 'or maybe it's the donkeys. I'm probably allergic to them. Or allergic to *you*,' she couldn't resist adding, at the same time averting her face, giving him the benefit of her flawless profile, heavily fringed eyes downcast.

As she turned away, a large hand came down on her shoulder and Mike's breath fanned her cheek as he said quietly, 'There's no need to be ashamed of your emotions, you know. Unless,' with a return to his sarcastic manner, 'you're afraid a few tears will ruin that porcelain complexion?'

Frankie stood very still. For a moment her legs seemed incapable of movement. There was something about the weight of his hand, the warm, wholesome breath that, for a fleeting moment, had assailed her nostrils. Damn it, the man actually seemed to exude an *aura*. An aura of what? But she knew the answer to that. Vibrant sexuality. With a sudden resurgence of strength, she jerked away from him.

'Is that it?' she asked coldly. 'Have we finished here?'

It seemed they had, apart from turning the animals out into the paddocks, a daily ritual, according to Mike, except in bad weather.

'They have to be brought in every night,' he warned. 'Donkeys are very susceptible to cold and wet.'

'How on earth did Aunt Francesca get into this?' an exasperated Frankie asked.

'She began with a couple of donkeys of her own. Just because she liked them. Then she saw an item in the local newspaper about a man being prosecuted for injuring his animal. She contacted the RSPCA and offered the animal a home with her own.'

'But the rest of them——?'

'Before you could say "hee-haw", she found herself with half a dozen. And then it just snowballed. Everyone who heard of a badly treated donkey immediately thought of your aunt. Or people who'd bought them as pets and found they couldn't cope. She could never refuse anyone—or rather she could never refuse a donkey. On the whole I think she preferred them to people. And even you must admit they are appealing little creatures.'

They were, with their soft warm muzzles and beautiful trusting eyes. But Frankie was careful not to show any signs of softening. This man struck her as the kind to take advantage of any form of weakness.

'You should have seen them with old Francesca,' Mike went on. 'They used to follow her about, for all the world like great shaggy dogs. As you may have gathered, I was extremely fond of your aunt. An indomitable old lady.'

Frankie, though busy divesting herself of the unflattering overall, was very aware of him studying her profile. 'You know,' he went on, 'you have quite a look of her.'

'Old? Or indomitable?' she enquired haughtily. He was altogether too damned familiar for someone she'd met only an hour ago.

'Oh, indomitable, of course. But perhaps in your case it's just plain cussedness?' And before she could expel the indignant breath, 'No, I shouldn't think you're any great age, are you? Nineteen? Twenty?'

'Twenty-two, actually.'

'Hmm. Must be due to keeping those lines at bay. By your age, most women are beginning to show a bit of character.'

Frankie stopped in mid-stride and glared up at him. That remark had been decidedly two-edged. It annoyed her still further that she had to tilt her head such a long way to confront him.

'Are you always this insulting?' she demanded. 'Or am I a special case?'

He had stopped when she did and now he looked down at her. At first she thought he was considering how to answer her question, maybe even contemplating an apology. But no. That, evidently, was too much to hope for.

'Oh, definitely a special case,' he drawled and there was something in his gaze that made her draw a fast, impeded breath. But then he went on with a reversion to his harsher manner, 'I'm trying to see just what you're made of. Whether or not you have any redeeming features. I can't believe that a girl with even the most diluted drop of old Francesca's blood in her veins could be so spineless as to ignore the challenge, to chuck away the chance of doing something so splendidly worthwhile.'

It was the word 'spineless' that caught Frankie on the raw, reminding her unpleasantly of her father and of Aunt Francesca's opinion of him.

'I am *not* spineless,' she snapped. 'Don't you dare level *that* accusation at *me*, you. . .you. . .arrogant bastard! You think you know such a hell of a lot about me, don't you? OK, so I *do* like to look and feel good.

But I can't see anything wrong with taking a pride in one's appearance.' Scornfully, 'It certainly wouldn't do *you* any harm.' Distastefully she eyed his faded jeans, now splashed with bran and coated with hair left by the affectionate attentions of the donkeys. 'And yes, I do enjoy my career. It's a very fulfilling one, which I'm not prepared to throw up in favour of mud and muck and a few filthy old donkeys. And nothing you can say will make me change my mind. Not that you've the *right* to say anything. Also, I'm. . . What are you doing?' she gasped, as a hard hand grasped her elbow and she found herself being forcibly urged towards the house at a faster pace than the oversize wellingtons could cope with.

Once she stumbled and would have fallen but for the inexorable strength supporting but still propelling her.

'What the hell do you think you're doing?' she repeated.

'I'm about to teach you a very necessary lesson—I hope,' was the grim reply.

CHAPTER TWO

DESPITE Frankie's struggles and her violent protests, Mike did not release her until they were back in the house. Then he kicked the door shut behind him and indicated one of the chairs, set at the large kitchen table.

'Sit down!'

He might have been talking to a recalcitrant dog, Frankie thought resentfully, and she ignored the directive. This man towered intimidatingly over her as it was. Seated she would be at even more of a disadvantage. But her motives were misinterpreted.

'But of course,' he jeered, 'I was forgetting. There's nowhere fit for milady to sit.' He grabbed the nearest thing to hand, the discarded overall, and made an ostentatious display of dusting the seat. 'Now,' he said, his hands forcefully on her shoulders, in a gesture that brooked no argument, 'sit there. There's something I want to show you.'

He moved across to the vast Welsh dresser that occupied the whole of one wall. With the ease of obvious familiarity, he pulled open a drawer and took out a manila folder which he slapped down on the table in front of Frankie. 'Go on,' he ordered, 'take a look.'

Wonderingly, she opened it, to see her own face staring up at her in a multiplicity of expressions. She began to leaf through dozens of pages cut from news-papers or from glossy magazines. On one or two of them there were pencilled notes in what must be her aunt's handwriting. 'My god-daughter', and in one case, 'My Frankie gets more and more beautiful'.

'See how much—and how often—she thought of you,' Mike said as he sat down facing her. 'She guarded those pictures as if they were gold. Every time she had a new one, she would show me—and with such pride. I know your face as well as I know my own. And not only your face!' he added drily as the folder revealed a seductive bikini pose. 'Then out would come all the old stories about you. You know the way old folk are? The way they love to reminisce. Pity that was all she had of you—photographs and memories.'

But he didn't need to tell her that. At the thought of her aunt, living her solitary existence with only animals for company, making this collection and hoarding it so carefully, Frankie's eyes filled with tears for the second time that day.

'I'd no idea,' she whispered brokenly. She looked up at Mike, lips trembling. 'I *wanted* to come and see her. I wanted to so much, but I couldn't hurt my mother.' A short while ago she had denied his right to an explanation, but now she found herself telling him the details of her mother's quarrel with her great-aunt. 'And,' she concluded, 'it didn't make Mum any more forgiving because Auntie was right about my father.'

But even this excuse did not move this grim-faced man. 'You could have come after your mother's death.'

'Yes.' Frankie sighed. 'But I've been so busy.

Modelling is very demanding work. I honestly thought there'd be plenty of time.'

'Well, you were wrong. Time ran out for old Francesca,' Mike said harshly. 'And you didn't even come to her funeral.'

'I didn't know she'd died,' Frankie said. 'The first I knew of it was when I got the solicitor's letter. I *would* have come if I'd known. Oh, I wish——'

'No good wishing, but you could *still* make amends—of a kind,' Mike told her.

Frankie looked up at him. Her green eyes, still bright with tears, were puzzled. 'How?'

'By doing what she wanted you to do. Take over this place.'

Frankie shook her head. 'No. I couldn't. I don't understand how she thought I could. Not when she knew about all this.' She indicated the cuttings.

'Maybe she thought—as I do—that all *this*——' he flicked the cuttings with a dismissive finger '—can't last forever. Oh, come on, Frankie, face facts. You're young and beautiful now—very beautiful.' He said it grudgingly. 'You're vivid, voluptuous.' His eyes scanned her body. 'But photographers' models are ten a penny. The public is fickle. Tastes change. And your beauty won't last forever. Character does—if you have any. You never know, you could be happier, in the long run, leading the simple life.'

At his unwilling compliment colour had scorched her skin. But it faded quickly at his unpalatable forecast. 'Even if all that were true,' Frankie said, 'which I don't believe, there's no way my fiancé would let me——'

'Fiancé?' Mike spoke sharply. 'You're engaged?'

Before she could guess his intention, he had leaned across the table and picked up her left hand. 'Since when? I don't see any ring. And there's been nothing in the Press or Francesca would have had that on file too.'

Frankie felt once more that disturbing but unwanted sensation at the touch of his hand—almost as though his flesh had burned hers—and hastily withdrew her fingers from his clasp. 'We've been engaged six months,' she told him, 'but we haven't made an announcement, or bought the ring yet.'

'Why?' he enquired bluntly.

'Nigel thinks it's more important to save up, for our future.'

'Tight-fisted, is he?'

Frankie glared at him. 'Certainly not!' And Nigel *wasn't* mean, she thought, just a little. . .a little careful. And after her father's spendthrift ways that was a decided point in his favour.

'But you're both earning?'

'Yes, at the moment, but Nigel says that after we're married. . .' She broke off. What was she doing, discussing her relationship with Nigel with this man? 'It's none of your business anyway,' she told him.

'Let me guess anyhow. It's my bet Nigel's said you're to give up work once you're married.'

'He'd prefer it, certainly,' Frankie said stiffly, remembering unwillingly certain recent disagreements.

'I can see why he would,' Mike mused. His dark eyes were busy, making another of their impertinent assessments, and suddenly Frankie felt as naked as when she posed for underwear shots. 'If you were *my* wife, I don't think I'd like to see your lovely body plastered all over advertisement hoardings.'

Nigel had actually said something along those lines, but Frankie was not about to admit it, nor that they had argued over the subject. She stood up.

'I suppose I may as well look over the rest of the house while I'm here.' She pulled a face. 'I hope it's not as bad as this kitchen.'

'You won't find much,' Mike warned, rising with her, 'except the basic essentials. Old Francesca didn't go in for luxuries or personal possessions. So if you're expecting to find a few heirlooms you can sell off, forget it.'

Because that was just what she had been contemplating, Frankie blushed scarlet. But the fact that Mike had only hit on the truth did not make her any less furious with him.

'I do wish you'd mind your own business,' she muttered.

She would have liked to make the tour of inspection alone. But Mike seemed determined to accompany her and to continue his pressurising, the appeal to her emotions.

'Stay, Frankie,' he urged. 'Give it a try. Your aunt wanted that more than anything. She was a great woman. As I told you, I was very fond of her and her death hasn't changed that.' And, as Frankie looked at him questioningly, he went on, his tone charged with unmistakable emotion, 'Wherever heaven is, I believe she's there, watching us. And lord knows I owe her a great deal. If I could convince you to stay, I'd feel as though I'd paid at least part of my debt to her.'

Frankie was a little disconcerted by his frankness. She had a personal faith, but it was a quiet, private thing. And Nigel, though he dutifully escorted his mother to church, was not religious by inclination. He would never have spoken of heaven in that way, as though it were simply another country whose existence was beyond dispute. To cover her embarrassment she was flippant.

'I would have thought it was the other way around—that *she* owed *you*.'

'You're talking about veterinary bills, of course. I'm talking about something entirely different. Maybe I'll tell you about it some day.' And Frankie couldn't be bothered to protest at the unlikeliness of his having an opportunity.

As she went from room to room she became more and more depressed. 'However could Auntie Fran live like this? It must have cost her an arm and a leg to feed all those wretched donkeys. Why didn't she spend a bit on her own comfort?'

'Believe me, I suggested it once or twice but she was happy going her own way. But I agree, if *you're* going to live here, some improvements will have to be made. You're a different kettle of fish altogether. I don't suppose you've been accustomed to roughing it.'

The implied criticism made Frankie turn on him with more venom than she might otherwise have employed. 'Are you thick? Or are you just being deliberately obtuse? There's no way I can live in this house. I have to be near London, for my work. And in any case my fiancé would never agree to our moving right out here.

Apart from the fact that he dislikes the country, it would be too far from his mother.'

The widowed Mrs Greaves claimed to be in poor health and Nigel had once suggested that, after they were married, they could share his mother's house.

'It's a great rambling place,' he had said, 'plenty of room for all three of us—and for kids if and when they come along.'

But Frankie had seen too many marriages founder on the rocks of in-law problems. Nor did she fancy Mrs Greaves taking a hand in raising *her* children. She wanted a home of her own, however modest, and not necessarily in Potters Bar, even though it was handy for commuting to London.

Mike guffawed. 'Never marry a mummy's boy. It's death to a marriage.'

'I didn't say he was a. . . oh, what's the use? You're just determined to be obnoxious.'

'No,' he denied, 'but I am determined about one thing. I've kept things ticking over here until the rightful owner turned up. But I'm a busy man. I shouldn't be here right now. I have a practice to run. So it's over to you.' He made a move towards the door.

'Oh, no, you don't!' Frankie exclaimed. She grabbed at his arm. Then, as an odd expression crossed his face, she released it just as hastily. 'Just you hold on a minute. You're not the only one with a job to get back to. I'm leaving here myself shortly. And even if I weren't, I couldn't possibly look after twenty donkeys on my own.'

'Your aunt managed,' he pointed out unsympathetically.

'But I know nothing about——'

'You could learn.'

Frankie stamped her foot. 'I have no desire to learn. I——'

'So you'll just drive off into the blue, will you?' he demanded scathingly. 'Back to the world of glamour and vanity and leave the poor creatures to starve?'

Frankie knew she couldn't. 'That's unfair. It's emotional blackmail. Besides, *you* wouldn't let them——'

'Frankie.' Curtly, he interrupted her. 'However little you like the idea, those donkeys are now *your* responsibility. I will only attend them when they get sick. Good lord, woman,' he demanded, 'have you nothing of your aunt in you? She adored her animals. It's a pity there aren't more like her.'

'Yes,' Frankie said with angry sarcasm, 'I bet she was a good source of income for you. All those donkeys, needing treatment every five minutes. I suppose you'll be putting in quite a hefty bill for recent services.'

His expression became closed. 'As it happens, the estate *does* owe me a considerable amount of money for the past couple of weeks. Money I *was* prepared to waive in the circumstances. But no longer.'

'Right!' Frankie snapped. 'Go, then! And you can render your rotten bill as soon as you like. You'll get your money. But I'll send it. Don't bother to call. If I never have to set eyes on you again, it will be too soon.'

Frankie had never considered herself to be the weepy type, but for the third time that day Mike had brought her close to tears. It wasn't fair. She hadn't asked her aunt to leave her anything. And to be lumbered with a grotty old house and what now seemed like hundreds of donkeys. Could Mike really be so unfeeling as to go off and leave her, when she hadn't the faintest idea of what she was supposed to do?

He gave her a long speculative look. Then, with a sigh of irritation, he sat down again at the table, cleared a space, pulled a notebook out of his shirt pocket and began to scribble furiously. After a few moments he stood up and thrust several small sheets of paper towards her. 'Here you are.'

'What's that?'

'A list of what needs doing and when.' This time he did not stop at the door but opened it and strode out into the yard.

'You're. . .you're really going?' Frankie said disbelievingly. She followed him out to his Land Rover. She had told him to go, told him she never wanted to see him again. But. . .

'Correct!' But having started the engine he did not immediately drive away. 'Look,' he said, 'my number's in the book if you get in a mess.' He sounded as if it was inevitable, and Frankie's chin rose a couple of inches, her eyes cold, glittering emeralds.

'If you drive away from here, hell may freeze over before I call you,' she told him. 'There must be other vets.'

'Not within a fifty-mile radius.' He looked worried. Afraid she might take substantial business elsewhere, Frankie thought scornfully. 'Look,' he said again, 'there's no love lost between us; I knew even before I set eyes on you there wouldn't be, the sort of woman you are. But for pity's sake don't let pride stand in your way. If one of the donkeys is in trouble, send for me.'

The sort of woman you are! Frankie clenched her teeth on a most unladylike retort. When she did not answer, his frown deepened.

'Look, a couple of those mares are in foal. Lord knows when they'll decide to drop. But you can bet your life it will be at the most inconvenient time.'

'Don't you know?' Frankie sneered. 'You're the vet.'

His hands clenched on the steering-wheel but he answered quietly. 'They were pregnant when your aunt took them on. She had no idea when they were mated. The gestation period can be anything between eleven and thirteen months. Nothing might happen for weeks or it could be tonight. Oh, to hell with it.' He shrugged fatalistically. 'I've warned you, dammit. So unless your *talents* happen to include midwifery——'

'Which they don't.'

'Then call me, damn you!' He accelerated away.

Somehow Frankie got through the next few hours. Luckily, she'd had the foresight to bring a small overnight bag with her and her first task was to make one of the untenanted bedrooms reasonably habitable. It was as well she did, for by the time she had worked her way through Mike's list of donkey-related chores, she had just about enough strength to climb the stairs before collapsing into bed.

This was the most ridiculous situation. Only a few hours' drive away she had a rewarding job and a warm, comfortable flat. Instead, here she was in a cold damp house, miles from anywhere, and all day she had been skivvying like some farm labourer.

But even when she *was* in bed, sleep seemed to elude her. With her eyes closed she could see Mike's face—all too vividly—hear his accusing voice. *Was* he as ugly as she'd at first decided? There was something in his features, rugged as they were, which compelled and fascinated.

Oh, what the hell! What did it matter if Mike was attractive or downright hideous? It was Nigel who should be occupying her thoughts right now. Nigel who *was* handsome with his golden hair and blue eyes. Nigel who, frustratingly, was out of reach.

A telephone call to Potters Bar had elicited the grudging information from Mrs Greaves that Nigel was now in Edinburgh and no, she didn't know when he'd be back or how Frankie could contact him.

'It's all right for you,' she told the donkeys next morning when they brayed a greeting as she struggled towards them with their mash. 'Anyone will do for you, so long as they feed you.'

But, despite herself, it was impossible not to feel flattered when her hand was nuzzled or a velvety muzzle rested on her shoulder and great liquid eyes met hers in palpable adoration.

'Cajolery will get you nowhere,' she told them but with only a half-hearted shove at hairy shoulders.

Mike had judged her correctly when he'd more or less dared her to go off and leave these hapless creatures to their fate. Frankie just could not do it.

'But I'm still not spending the rest of my life looking

after you,' she told one particularly appealing choc-olate-coloured mare who seemed to have taken a fancy to her. 'So you can cut out the flannel.'

Rather than endure another chilly conversation with her future mother-in-law, Frankie snatched a few odd moments in the middle of the day to go down to the village and post a letter to Nigel.

Despite her gloomy mood she had to admit that Lionswick was probably very attractive in summer, with its small picture-book cottages, set individually or built in rows, every stone of their walls a different subtle shade of golden grey.

Walking from her parked car to the post office, she passed a gateway bearing a brass plate. 'Michael J. Leeming, Veterinary Surgeon.' So that was his sur-name. Leeming! The name sounded familiar, but she could not think why. And this was where he conducted his practice. She presumed he also lived in the large house she could just see at the far end of the drive.

By the end of the day she was exhausted again. But tonight she was not to have an uninterrupted sleep. That night one of the pregnant mares decided to drop her foal.

It seemed to Frankie that her head had only just touched the pillow when the noise began. At first she tried to ignore it, but finally conscience dragged her from her bed. Pulling an old raincoat of her aunt's over her flimsy nightdress, she staggered sleepily out into the cold of the stableyard. Several of the animals seemed to be in a disturbed condition. Later, she was to realise the almost telepathic communication between the little family groups, the way they brayed for help when one of their number was in trouble.

She finally located the centre of the disturbance, a gentle-natured mare. It was obvious even to Frankie's inexperienced eye that she was about to give birth.

'Oh, heavens, *now* what do I do?' But there was only one answer. As Mike had pointed out, at times like this there was no room for personal pride or resentment. Frankie ran back to the house.

A woman answered the telephone—his wife, Frankie supposed, and was surprised at a totally illogical stab of disappointment. Heavens, what did it matter to her whether or not Mike Leeming was married? The woman sounded as sleepy as Frankie had felt until a few moments ago.

'I'm afraid Mike's not here. He's been called out to a sick cow. Is it urgent?' And when a breathless Frankie had detailed the situation and her own inexperience, 'I'll try and get in touch with him. Just do the best you can till he gets there. Quite often animals manage very well on their own.'

Ordinarily, Frankie was no coward, but she felt badly frightened as she rushed back to the stable. Suppose the donkey *couldn't* manage? Suppose the foal died, or the mother died? She knew very well who would get the blame. She hoped Mike's wife was more reliable than Nigel's mother about passing on messages.

The moment she regained the stable it was obvious that all was not well. The donkey was lying on her side, deeply distressed. Frankie dropped to her knees in the straw by the mare's head. 'Oh, please don't die on me,' she begged.

Each of her aunt's animals wore a strong collar bearing a disc with its name. Frankie fumbled to find it. 'Lucky,' she read. 'Oh, Lucky, I hope you live up to your name.'

Whether it was the comforting sound of a human voice, Frankie could not be sure, but the beast seemed less restless. So, despite her own cold discomfort, she stayed where she was, talking to it as the difficult birth progressed.

'I'm sure that's not right, Lucky,' she was saying a little later. 'I don't know much about babies, but surely the legs don't come first.'

'They do!' a deep voice interrupted her monologue. 'But it should be the forelegs, not the hindlegs.'

'Oh, Mike!' Frankie leaped to her feet. All animosity temporarily forgotten, she could have hugged him, she was so relieved to see him. 'Thank goodness your wife gave you the message.' She thought he gave her an odd look but he said nothing, giving all his attention to the donkey.

'If you're at all squeamish,' he said, 'you'd better leave me to it.'

'Oh, but I'm not,' she assured him.

It was an extremely intricate task, extricating the breech-presented foal, and despite her dislike of him Frankie watched, in breathless admiration of Mike's skill, the tenderness combined with strength with which he handled the animal.

'There we are,' he said at last. He put the wet little creature by its mother who immediately began to lick the bedraggled coat. 'What are you going to call her?

How about Frankie?' he suggested, then, 'Good heavens, woman, what are you crying for?'

Shamefacedly, Frankie rubbed her hands over her eyes. 'I expect it's the relief. I was really worried. I thought they were both going to die.' But she knew there was more to it than that. It had been an incredibly moving experience to be present at the beginning of a new life.

'Well, there's no need to worry. They'll both be fine now.' To Frankie's everlasting astonishment, Mike put an arm about her shoulders. 'I'm glad you had the sense to send for me.' Then, as she shuddered convulsively, 'Good lord, woman, you're frozen. And no wonder. You've precious little on under that thin raincoat.'

She *was* cold, but it wasn't just the night-time chill which had made her shiver, but his very masculine proximity. And Frankie was well aware of the scantiness of her clothing. Whatever has got into you? she scolded herself. Allowing a virtual stranger—a man you don't even like—to disturb you like this?

'What you need is a hot drink!' Mike said, and Frankie found herself being steered back to the house, that large arm still about her. 'Though it'll be a miracle if there's anything suitable in the kitchen cupboard.'

'I bought some hot chocolate today in the village.' She had been relieved, too, to find a couple of small stores where she could purchase not only a hot-water bottle but also a pair of jeans and a warm sweater. Her overnight bag had not included clothes suitable for feeding and mucking out donkeys.

As they neared the house, she slipped free of Mike's encircling arm and faced him, blocking the doorway.

'Goodnight, Mike, and thanks. Another bill for you to put in.'

'Good lord!' He sounded exasperated. 'Don't *I* get to have a drink? I've been out nearly all night, and it's as cold as charity.'

'Don't you have hot chocolate at home?'

'Yes.' He was looking her up and down in a very odd way. 'But no one nearly so attractive to make it for me.'

'I wouldn't let your wife hear you say that,' she retorted.

'I don't have a wife.' Firmly he set Frankie to one side, leaving her to follow him into the kitchen. 'So you don't have to worry about my reputation.'

His reputation? What about hers? What on earth would Nigel say if he could see the two of them now? And why, for heaven's sake, did she suddenly feel so elated? It couldn't possibly be anything to do with the fact that Mike was not married. That didn't make sense. 'So who answered the phone?' she asked.

'My mother.'

'So now who's a mummy's boy?' she taunted.

'Not me,' he said deflatingly. 'My mother is only staying for a couple of weeks, while her own house is being redecorated. And since she's getting on a bit she won't be waiting up for me. So how about that hot chocolate?' And Frankie found herself complying, while, without waiting for an invitation, he sat himself down at the table.

'You seem to have coped very well so far,' he

observed as she hunted for a couple of reasonably clean mugs. 'Your *aunt* thought you would.' His tone implied that he had not shared that optimism.'

'I've only managed because you left me no choice.' She regarded him earnestly. Somehow she must make him see sense. 'Mike, I've changed from the child my aunt remembered. Yes, I loved to visit her and I did enjoy helping her—but she only had dogs and cats in those days—oh, and a nanny goat.' For an instant a reminiscent smile lit her green eyes. 'I even learned to milk the goat. But I've *changed*.'

'I don't believe it.' As she put his drink down in front of him, his hand closed over hers and again that wave of physical awareness swept over her, so that she found it difficult to follow what he was saying. 'Basically, you know, people *don't* change. OK, you may have buried your love of the countryside and animals under a veneer of city sophistication. But underneath you're still the same person.' As a bemused Frankie withdrew her hand he leaned back. 'Will you call the foal Frankie?'

'I hadn't even thought about it,' she lied, for the idea had rather appealed to her. 'There doesn't seem much point really.'

His manner, which tonight had been friendlier than on the last occasion they'd met, changed abruptly. 'So you're still determined not to stay.'

'That's right. Oh, you needn't glare at me like that. I'll see the donkeys are looked after until their future is decided on. But I'm putting this place up for sale and going back to town.' Somehow saying it did not give her as much satisfaction as she had expected.

She slumped in her chair, hands tightly clasped around the mug of hot chocolate. She needed its comfort. Lucky's emergency had banished all thoughts of tiredness. But now that the surge of adrenalin had receded she felt both weary and depressed by her impossible situation and—she had to admit it—by the disapproval of this man. Though why it should matter to her what Mike Leeming thought she couldn't imagine.

'You can't sell this place,' Mike said with such assurance that Frankie looked curiously at him.

'Of course I can. I——'

'No.' He shook his head. 'It's part of the terms of the will. You can't sell and you can't get rid of the donkeys.'

Frankie stared at him blankly for a few seconds, unable to take in what he had said. Then, 'I don't believe you,' she muttered. 'The solicitor didn't say. . . This is one of your attempts to——'

'No. What would be the point of lying?' He leaned forward across the table. 'You forget, I was your aunt's friend and privy to her wishes. What the solicitor was *not* instructed to tell you—because that was to be left to *me*—is that this place is to remain a donkey sanctuary, whatever *you* decide to do.'

'You mean——?'

'I mean that if you stay on and run it as your aunt wished, you also get the money to do so, plus a considerable sum for yourself. You seem to be under the impression that your aunt was poor. Far from it, I assure you.'

'But *why* didn't the solicitor——?'

'Because that's what your aunt decided—after discussing it with me.'

'Discussing it with *you*?' Frankie was indignant. 'What's it got to do——?'

'I guess she was secretly afraid you'd turn out to be more your father's daughter than your mother's. You were to be given a chance to show your mettle. Coercion was only to be applied if necessary.'

'*Coercion*?' Frankie couldn't believe what she was hearing.

'An appeal to your mercenary side, if you like. You see, if you refuse to live here and go on running this place as a sanctuary, you don't get a penny.'

Frankie leaned forward across the table, unaware in her agitation of the parted lapels of the raincoat, the excellent view she was affording him of swelling, creamy breasts, rising and falling in her angry anxiety. 'I don't believe it. You *are* lying. You must be. I'll see the solicitor again. There must be something I can do about it.'

'No.' Again he shook his head. 'It's all tied up right and tight. All legal and above board. You don't get a penny. And the place will be run by a trustee.'

'A trustee?' Suddenly the penny dropped. Suddenly she remembered why the name Leeming had struck a chord. 'That's *you*, isn't it?' she demanded angrily. '*You're* the trustee?'

CHAPTER THREE

'YES, I'm the trustee.'

Frankie jumped to her feet, glaring down at Mike. 'I might have known! That settles it. I shall definitely consult a solicitor—a different one. I'll claim undue influence. Somehow you wormed your way into my aunt's confidence and——'

'Hold on! Hold on!' Mike too had risen and now he came round the table, hands outstretched, their purpose all too obvious.

'Don't touch me! Don't you dare!' Frankie backed away but forgot the chair and as she stumbled his fingers clamped down on her shoulders, painfully hard through the thin raincoat. Painfully hard and yet. . .and yet the discomfort went unheeded as every warning instinct throbbed into life.

'Touch you!' He spoke through clenched teeth and she suddenly realised how furiously angry he was. 'I'd like to give you a damned good shaking! You want to think before you speak, my girl. Before you start hurling your unwarranted accusations.'

'Unwarranted! Huh!' Inwardly, Frankie was quaking, not only at his anger but at his nerve-racking proximity, but she would not let him sense that. Her green eyes blazed at him. You've condemned yourself out of your own mouth. You said my aunt consulted you about her plans, about the terms of her will. You *inveigled* your way into becoming her trustee. And now you think you can manipulate *me*. Well, you can't. I——'

'Shut up! Shut up and listen for a minute.'

'I won't listen!' Despite the hands on her shoulders Frankie managed to raise her hands and clap them over her ears. 'You've got nothing to say that will interest me. You can say it to the lawyers—in court! I. . . Why, you—you brute! Let *go* of me!'

For Mike had given way to his declared impulse and was shaking her so violently that her rattling teeth trapped her still-busy tongue, giving it a painful bite, bringing tears to her eyes.

'Never in my whole life,' Mike roared, 'has anyone ever dared to accuse me——'

'Why? Because you might turn rough?' she mumbled painfully. It was the wrong line to take. Especially when his temper was already on a short fuse.

'Don't you ever learn?' His dark eyes bored into her upturned defiant ones. With Mike there was always a constant impalpable sense of danger and suddenly she realised that he was too close for comfort and that he was a whole lot of man—perhaps too much for her to handle. Their disagreement was getting far too personal. It wasn't so much that she was afraid of his becoming violent, but that she was far too aware of him as a man. And it was the last thing she wanted.

'Let go of me,' she repeated, 'You great overbearing——'

'Don't you know when to shut your mouth?' Mike demanded. Something dark and frightening flickered in the dark eyes, then, 'Well, I know one good way of shutting it for you!' And before she could guess at and foil his intention his dark head swooped down, all masculine predation. The combination of his hard lips on hers and the sensation of being crushed against a broad ribcage drove every vestige of breath from Frankie's quivering body.

After that first startled, disbelieving instant, she began to fight, pummelling with her hands against his shoulders and, when that was of no avail, she administered a kick to his shins. But since she was still wearing her aunt's unwieldy wellingtons, the kick was ineffective.

The punishing kiss seemed to go on and on. It had not begun as a kiss but as a means of shutting her up and she resented it as such. But somewhere along the way Frankie's emotions seemed to change. However, just as she felt on the verge of collapse, Mike released her, and when at last he loosened his hold, so violently that she fell back on the hard wooden chair, Frankie had to take a deep breath before she could speak.

'You. . .you. . .'

He was breathing heavily, his face was flushed and his eyes glittering. His hands were balled now into fists at his side. 'You stupid, brainless little fool. If you had anything in your head besides promoting your own charms, you'd realise that your accusations make no sense. I'm your aunt's trustee, yes. But I've derived no benefit from it—just a lot of damned hard work. Work that I look like being lumbered with for a long time yet, since you're stubbornly determined not to face your responsibilities.'

'No benefit?' Frankie was just able to mumble disbelievingly. Her mouth still stung from that assault of a kiss. 'So what happens to all the money, then. If *I* don't get it?'

'It goes to pay the wages of whoever has to run this place in your stead. Not to *me*, as you tried to insinuate.'

'Even so, you. . .you had no right to treat me like that.' Frankie's voice shook as she struggled to regain her poise and she knew she dared not risk standing up just yet. Her legs felt as though they did not belong to her.

'Maybe not,' he said grimly. 'But it had the desired effect, didn't it? It kept you quiet long enough for me to put you straight on a few things. And now I'm going home to my bed. I'd advise you to do the same. You'll have to be up in a few hours to do morning feeds.'

Frankie did go back to bed, but her tumultuous thoughts would not let her sleep. Mike Leeming was a bully. How dared he treat her that way? Frustrated rage filled her as she thought of the things she would have liked to say to him—to do to him. Lord, how she loathed him. And yet—and this made her angrier than anything else—if he had not released her when he had, Frankie knew she would have responded to that merciless kiss. But had it meant anything to *him*? No way. Or if it had he certainly hadn't shown it.

Finally, in exasperation, because it was easier to combat troublesome thought with action, she got up again and gave twenty surprised but appreciative donkeys an early breakfast.

The new arrival was doing well, suckling strongly,
she noted with relief. She returned to the stable several
times during the morning, unable to quell an almost
maternal pride in the little foal. She really was an
endearing little mite. Unlike her jet-black mother, the
foal was an attractive dapple grey.

'Whoever your father was, Frankie, he must have
been an attractive-looking fellow.'

'Talking to yourself?'

At the sarcastic enquiry, Frankie swung round,
colour staining her cheeks, furious at having to admit
to her ridiculous occupation. But that was better than
letting him think she *was* indulging in self-
congratulation.

'I was talking to the donkey.' It was difficult to meet
his eyes, but from *his* manner, Frankie thought indignantly, last night might never have happened. Here he
was, acting as cool as a cucumber, while she. . .she was
filled with acute embarrassment, remembering all too
vividly that kiss. A kiss *he* had intended to be a
punishment. But which, for her, had very nearly
become something else—something far more disturbing. 'And what are *you* doing here?' she snapped. 'I'm
surprised you have the nerve to show your face after
last night.'

'Last night?' He sounded puzzled as though he had
absolutely no idea of what she meant. Then his brows
rose quizzically. 'Oh, *that*! Don't worry, Frankie, it's
not something I intend to repeat. I didn't derive any
satisfaction from it—any more than you did.'

She would not have believed him if he had pretended

otherwise. She knew very well that he did not like her. Nevertheless, the truth hurt.

'So what *do* you want?' she demanded.

'I've come to check up on little Frankie, of course. I gather you've decided to call her that?' Mockingly, 'I'm surprised you didn't reject the suggestion out of hand—since it came from me.'

Frankie did not even deign to answer. She turned on her heel and stalked back towards the house, feeling badly in need of a strong cup of coffee.

'Mother and daughter both doing well!' Mike put his head round the back door to report. Then, seeing her occupation, 'I'll join you in that coffee. I've got another six calls to make, so I doubt if I'll get any lunch.'

'Tough!' Frankie said unsympathetically, but already he was seating himself at the table. If it were not for a change of clothes, he might never have moved since last night.

'Needs decorating, doesn't it?' He was looking around the kitchen. 'I expect the whole house does. Guess I never really noticed before. I could recommend a couple of reliable——'

'No, thanks!' Frankie slapped a mug down in front of him. 'Nothing's changed. I still haven't said I'm staying. I told you, I'm going to take legal advice—and I meant it.'

He was infuriatingly unperturbed. 'And *I* tell *you*—again—you'd be wasting your time. It won't do any good. The only way you'll get your hands on your aunt's money——'

'Is that all you think I'm interested in?'

'Well, isn't it?'

'No, I——' She broke off then, because she was essentially truthful. 'Well, yes. I admit the money would come in useful. It would mean Nigel and I could afford to get married now, instead of waiting another year. But it looks as though we'll just have to go on waiting. There's no way I can get married *and* live here. Nigel——'

'You know,' Mike interrupted, 'I'm not sure that I like the sound of this Nigel.'

'*You* aren't required to like him,' Frankie said frostily. 'But in any case that's a ridiculous remark. You've never met him. You don't know anything about him.'

'I know what I've gathered from you.'

But Frankie did not even need to search her conscience. She knew she would never have said anything derogatory about Nigel.

'You've deliberately misinterpreted me, then. Nigel is. . .is a good man.'

Mike's eyebrows rose sardonically and Frankie knew her defence of Nigel, however true, had been pitifully inadequate. 'And *shall* I have a chance to meet this paragon, then?' he asked.

'I've written and asked him to come down.'

'Wouldn't it have been quicker to telephone?'

'Yes,' Frankie said. Then added unwarily, 'If only I could trust his mother to pass on the message.'

Mike pounced. 'Ah-hah! Do I detect a case of a possessive mother?'

'She'd like to be,' Frankie admitted reluctantly. 'But once we're married. . .' Her voice trailed off at his sceptical look. 'Oh, I *do* wish you'd mind your own business,' she said crossly.

'Why? Because I'm uncomfortably close to the truth?' He leaned across the table and, as if he were not really aware of what he was doing, he took one of her hands in both of his, turning it over, playing with the long slim fingers as he fixed her with a sharp inquisitorial stare. 'You've said there's no way this Nigel would consider living here. And if you marry him——'

'I'll live wherever he wants to live, yes.' Except with his mother, she added the silent rider.

'And the donkeys?'

'Oh!' Exasperated, Frankie snatched away the hand which until then, for some inexplicable reason, she had let him retain. 'Damn the donkeys—and damn you. I wish you'd stop nagging me.'

'I'll have to, for the moment.' Ruefully, Mike showed her the time. 'I shall be getting stick from old Jed Spriggs as it is. I should have been at his farm an hour ago. But I'll be back. And,' he warned her, 'when I want something I don't give up that easily. And I want you to stay here.'

She could believe in his determination, Frankie thought, watching his now familiar back view as he strode towards his elderly Land Rover. She imagined that Mike could be quite ruthless if necessary. But, she told herself, domineering masculinity did not appeal to her. And it was ridiculous for him to be so anxious to keep her here. All right, granted he had had a rapport with her aunt and in his veterinary capacity he was concerned for the welfare of the animals. But she,

Frankie, was not essential to that welfare. Anyone would do. It was a surprisingly discouraging thought.

She did not return immediately to her chores. Instead she sat down again at the kitchen table and looked through her aunt's collection of photographs, studying each one carefully. Something Mike had said yesterday had been nagging at her ever since. *Were* the later ones as good as the earlier studies? Did her face still have the same quality advertisers sought to represent their products? Was she already losing her looks? Damn Mike Leeming for putting the doubt into her mind.

Then, angrily, she slapped the folder closed. You're *not* past it yet, she told herself. For heaven's sake don't let that man undermine your morale. And, more severely, don't let him undermine your feelings for Nigel. Though what she meant by that she wasn't exactly sure.

A couple of days later, there had still been no reply to her letter in which she had also asked Nigel to go to her flat and bring her a selection of clothes. And Frankie realised she would have to go into the nearest town to replenish her wardrobe. There wasn't time in an afternoon to go all the way to Potters Bar herself and still be back in time to bring the donkeys in for the night and feed them.

It was enjoyable—if only for a couple of hours—to discard her working clothes. Even though she only had the smart suit in which she had travelled down—was it really only a few days ago?

Having invested in another pair of jeans and a couple

more sweaters, as well as some much-needed underwear, she passed a DIY shop. There was a sale on. She had another half-hour to spare before she needed to get back and she wandered inside without any real conscious intent. Ten minutes later she emerged, a couple of large tins of emulsion paint added to her load. After all, she excused her impulsive buy, it wouldn't hurt to freshen up that awful kitchen. The unhygienic appearance of its steam-darkened walls was getting her down.

It was typical of her recent luck, Frankie thought ruefully, that her car, always so reliable in town, should choose a lonely country lane to let her down. Fortunately she did know how to change a wheel. But the last time she'd had a puncture the garage had done the job for her and the equipment mechanics had used to tighten the wheelnuts was so efficient that she had a struggle to undo them. But finally the spare was in place and a slightly less immaculate Frankie drove on, nearly an hour late for evening feeding time. Moreover it was dark now, which was going to make the task more difficult.

As she turned into the rutted drive she saw that the house and stableyard were ablaze with light. Burglars? Nothing worth stealing. Donkey-nappers? She had heard horrific stories of what could happen to stolen animals. Regardless of her own safety, she skidded to a halt and rushed to investigate.

It was a relief to see the familiar Land Rover standing in the yard, its lights trained full on the paddocks where Mike was just rounding up the animals. She called out to him and he strode towards her. In the headlights she saw his face, contorted with anger.

'Where the blazes have you been?'

Immediately, Frankie was on the defensive. 'To town, not that it's any of your business.'

'Not my business! How the hell do you think I felt when I got here and found your car gone, the place deserted, everywhere locked up and donkeys yelling for food? I thought you'd left for good. Instead of that you're "in town".' He was looking her over with disdain in his expression. 'Just look at you! The immaculate hairdo, the make-up, the way you're dressed. Those are the things that really matter to you, aren't they? You make yourself look desirable—on the outside. But I'll tell you this for free, Frankie, it's what's on the inside that matters.'

It was not for nothing that Frankie had red hair, and she felt her anger rising to meet his. 'I'm getting more than a little tired of you and your insults, your accusations,' she flared. 'I *told* you I wouldn't leave here until something was sorted out about the donkeys. And of course it was them you were concerned for, wasn't it? It never occurred to you that something might have happened to me. That I might have had an accident.'

His expression changed at once. 'Have you? Are you hurt?' He grasped her arm and scanned her face. 'What happened?'

He smelt of male, warm, erotic, and sudden raw sensation pierced the pit of Frankie's stomach. Angry with him, but even more furious with herself, her febrile reactions, she shook free of him. 'Nothing, as it happens. Apart from a flat tyre. But you could have

waited to find out, instead of jumping down my throat.'
Tense in every limb, she stalked past him to finish the
job he had begun, of driving the donkeys back to their
stables, disconcerted when he remained to help.

'You don't *have* to cope single-handed,' he told her
as they worked. 'There must be several unemployed
youngsters in the village who would give their eye-teeth
for a job here. You could well afford to pay a *couple* of
assistants out of what your aunt left for maintenance.'

'Then why the hell didn't *she* have someone to help
her?' Frankie demanded. Her mind was already in a
state of turmoil and the magnitude of the task, and the
thought of the elderly woman of whom she'd once been
so fond struggling alone in such primitive conditions,
made her feel even more depressed and guilty.

'Because she was an independent old so-and-so. A
capable countrywoman, not a city wimp. She loved the
work. It filled a need in her life that a family should
have supplied.' There it was again, whether he intended
it or not, that old note of accusation. And how dared
he call her a city wimp?

She wondered why it was that she and Mike had
conceived such an instant antipathy for each other. But
then she remembered that he had prejudged her,
before they'd even met.

'You don't need to stay now that I *am* back,' she told
him curtly.

'I know. Nevertheless I'm staying.'

'To see I do the job properly?' But he did not deign
to answer.

In an antagonistic silence, on Frankie's part at least,
they doled out the bran mixture. She was still seething

over his reception of her, the way he had put the donkeys' welfare before hers. It shouldn't matter. But it did.

'Look, Frankie,' Mike began, following her as she stalked back to the house, two empty pails in each hand.

'No, you look,' she swung round to face him, 'I've had enough of your lectures. I had every right to go into town this afternoon. I *needed* to. Because of the rash promise I made you, about not abandoning the donkeys to their fate, I was stuck here with hardly a stitch to wear.'

He came closer, one hand outstretched, and she backed away. For some reason his hostile greeting had really upset her and she was afraid that if he touched her again she might react even more violently. His hand dropped to his side and he scowled.

'I only wanted to apologise. OK, so I was a bit hasty. But I really thought you'd gone off without so much as a word to me.'

'Oh, don't worry,' she retorted. 'I'll see to it that you're the first to know when that day comes. I shall take great satisfaction——'

'*If* it comes, which I hope it——'

'No, *when!*' Frankie suddenly had the feeling that it was vital she get away from this place and back to one of sanity and reality. And it wasn't the house and the donkeys she was rejecting this time but the man who stood before her. It shouldn't matter to her that he had been more concerned about those damned donkeys than about her. But it did. And it just wasn't logical.

'Now come on,' Mike protested, 'don't make rash

decisions just because you're mad at me. I've said I'm sorry. What more can I say, or do?'

'Nothing,' she told him. 'You have altogether too much to say for yourself. And now I'm going inside, to unpack my shopping, have a bath and then a meal. And I thought *you* had a home to go to,' she said coldly as he seemed to be on the point of following her as usual.

'I don't like to leave you yet, not in this frame of mind.'

'I'm not going to drown myself,' she snapped, 'just because you——'

Unexpectedly, he grinned. It was the first time she'd seen him smile and the effect hit her like a blow to the solar plexus. How had she ever thought he was ugly? 'Good,' he chuckled, 'you haven't entirely lost your sense of humour.' And to her fury, because she hadn't been joking, he tucked a hand under her elbow. 'How about if you unpack and have your bath and I cook—for both of us?'

Still mentally reeling from the impact of that smile, Frankie felt panic skitter through her. His proposal, though delivered with great matter-of-factness, was fraught with too much intimacy for her present state of confusion. She shook her head.

'There isn't enough food. I wasn't expecting company.'

'All right.' He was cheerfully undismayed. 'I'll nip down to the chippy. I'll be back before——'

'Hasn't it penetrated your thick skull yet?' Her conflicting emotions made her snap at him. 'I'm not in the mood for——'

'. . .my company? I know. Which is why I have to stick around until you are.' Again that engaging crooked smile and Frankie shot a suspicious glance at him.

She was curious as to why Mike should suddenly bother to turn on the charm. Their encounters to date had revealed him as having an abrasive personality. Coldly she told him, 'I can't think why it matters.'

'Can't you?' For a long, strangely breathtaking moment he stared down into her eyes. Then his face became a bleak barrier, restraining any emotion. Slowly, 'No, perhaps you can't. I'm not sure that *I* know either.' And, with a return to his normally brisk manner, 'But I'll go and get the fish and chips anyway. I'll be about ten minutes.'

'And if I don't open the door?'

'Just try locking me out,' he said darkly.

Frankie, despite her fiery hair and volatile temper, had never considered herself to be the rebellious type. Quite the contrary. Over the years she had been accustomed to deferring to the will of others—first her mother and more recently Nigel—except in the matter of living with *his* mother. And on that point she *was* adamant.

To her, acquiescence with the wishes of others had always seemed synonymous with good manners and rebelling merely for the sake of asserting one's right to do so was childish.

But perhaps, she thought now, she had never before felt the necessity to rebel. Until she'd met Mike Leeming. For some reason which she could not fathom, he brought out a side of her nature of which she felt ashamed. At times he induced in her a seething, boiling frustration that needed some outlet. She *wanted* to pit her will against his—and win. But so far, in every encounter, she felt that she had come out the loser. Otherwise why was she still here in this benighted hole, doing manual work until she was fit to drop and until the slender hands that had sold gallons of creams and lotions were more suitable as an advert for sandpaper?

Well, there was one thing she could do. She could lock him out of her house—him and his fish and chips. On this satisfactory notion—and having suited action to thought—she went upstairs to take her bath.

In a house that made no concessions to modernity, the bathroom was a masterpiece of antiquity with its chipped enamel bath and ancient fittings. The copper gas cylinder which heated the bathwater terrified her each time she used it, with its hesitant and then violent explosion into life. But at least once it was going the water ran gloriously hot and Frankie wallowed unashamedly, ignoring the knowledge that Mike Leeming would soon be beating, ineffectually, on the back door.

In all probability, she gloated, she would not even hear him. The house was solidly built and the roar of the gas cylinder, the rush of water falling three feet into the bath, would drown out all sound.

She was quite right about the sound-deadening effect, which was why she was shocked into a state bordering on the cataleptic when the bathroom door opened and she saw Mike Leeming standing on the threshold.

For what seemed an appalling length of time, Frankie was incapable of either speech or action. But it could not have been as long as it seemed. For, as her hand shot out to grab the bathtowel that was not where it should have been—set ready on a nearby chair—Mike strode forward.

'Get out!' Her voice cracked on the words. She was afraid. But not of rape. Some deep-seated intuition told her that Mike, however roused, would not descend to that kind of brutality.

But his immediate attention, she discovered, was not for her body, cowering in a very un-Venuslike manner beneath the soap suds. Instead he made for the gas cylinder, switching it off before turning to glower down at her.

'Are you mad? Don't you know you should never have that thing going while you're actually in the bath? It's as old as the hills. It could explode, or you could be overcome by fumes. Damn it, woman, you haven't even got any ventilation.' With which he proceeded to open the window, letting in a blast of wintry night air.

'What are you trying to *do* to me?' Frankie demanded. 'Frighten me into a heart attack or *freeze* me to death? How the hell did you get in? And what do you think you're doing, marching in here like this?'

'I'll tell you what I'm doing.' He glowered down at her. 'Against considerable odds, I'm trying to do you a good turn. I come back, bringing you your supper, only to find the door locked against me. And when I do get in, I find you giving an imitation of a suicidal lobster. People have been known to pass out in water that hot.'

Frankie ignored this last remark. She had been

having really hot baths all her life and to no ill effect. But, 'If this is your idea of doing someone a good turn, I'd hate to be on the receiving end of one of your *bad* turns. And just how *did* you get in?' she demanded.

'I've got a key,' he said with a smugness he could not hide. 'Now, are you going to get out of there? Your supper's downstairs going cold.'

'Firstly,' Frankie snapped, 'if you've got a key to *my* house, I'll thank you to return it. I'm not having you waltzing in and out just as you please. Secondly, I'm not getting out of this bath with you watching me. And thirdly, you can take your fish and chips and——'

'Now, now! Language!' He was well aware of the embarrassment—and perhaps more—that her anger sought to disguise and his chuckle was pure masculine amusement.

To do him credit, Frankie thought with unwilling admiration, his choleric moods were short-lived. Which was more than could be said for her own, especially since he had made no move to leave but was instead holding out the wayward bathtowel. His manner unmistakably invited her to allow him to wrap it around her. He seemed to have entirely regained his good humour—probably from amusement at her expense. Frankie felt she must cut a ridiculous figure, still trying to conceal her rapidly cooling flesh beneath the fast-diminishing foam.

'Put that towel down on the chair, where it belongs,' she said, pronouncing each word separately and distinctly from between clenched teeth, 'and get out!'

To her surprise—and relief—he complied. Frankie listened intently, until she heard his retreating footsteps on the stairs, then she shot out of the bath. Her first action was to slam and lock the door, her second to close the window, the draught from which was raising goosebumps on her silky skin.

She would have liked to take her time towelling herself dry and rubbing in body lotion, to combat the toll the last few days had taken of her normally pampered body. But the unheated bathroom was now far too cold for such sybaritic practices. Instead she rubbed fiercely, pulled on the fleecy pyjamas and dressing-gown that had been among the day's purchases and went downstairs. Still in a militant mood, Frankie did not suppose for one moment that Mike would have extended his strategic withdrawal to actually leaving the house.

She was right. He hadn't. He was seated at the kitchen table. Through recent right of tenure it seemed to have become uniquely *his* territory. On the elderly gas cooker a battered kettle had just reached that promising sound described as 'singing', while the oven emitted an aroma that tantalised Frankie's nostrils, making her realise just how long it was since she had eaten.

'I had to warm them up again,' he greeted her cheerfully.

'I'd noticed.' Frankie was ironic. She noticed also, with slightly more gratitude, that he'd made use of his time to light the fire she'd set that morning.

'Sit down,' he invited. As if, Frankie fulminated, this were *his* house and she *his* guest. But she made no protest. She was beginning to realise that arguing with Mike Leeming was tantamount to beating one's head against a brick wall. She would satisfy her sudden, ravenous hunger, she thought cravenly, before taking issue with him about his most recent behaviour. With a full stomach and—comparatively—decently clad, she would feel better able to outface him. Why *did* she occasionally feel so nervous of him, when most of the time she thoroughly disliked and resented him?

So much for her decision to hold fire. 'Feeling better for your bath?' Either Mike had not expected a truce or he was being deliberately provocative. All right, if he *wanted* a fight. . .

'I would have done!' she snapped pointedly.

'Or you might have felt a whole lot worse.' He set a heaped plate of fish and chips before her. 'I meant what I said about that old copper geyser. One of the first improvements you ought to make to this house is to have a modern heating and plumbing system installed.'

'I'm not planning on *any* improvement,' Frankie paused long enough to say before taking the first blissful mouthful.

'Oh?' He looked pointedly at the two cans of emulsion paint which she had dumped on the dresser and forgotten.

'That's only for the kitchen,' Frankie demurred. 'I'd like it to look a little less insanitary before Nigel arrives, so that I can offer him a meal.'

Sharply, a chip halfway to his mouth, 'You've heard from him, then?'

'Not yet,' she was forced to admit. 'But it'll only be a matter of time.'

Mike relaxed and carried on eating. 'Not an over-eager fiancé, is he?'

'He might not have had my letter yet,' Frankie said defensively. 'He's away a lot.'

'What does he do?'

'He's a rep—a publisher's rep. It takes him all over the country.'

'I thought publishers had area reps?'

'It's only a small firm as yet. There's only Nigel and one other man. But it's expanding.'

'But not enough for him to be able to support a wife?'

'We've agreed—that on only one salary——'

'Oh? What's become of your "career" all of a sudden?'

Inwardly, Frankie cursed. That was something Mike was too good at, luring her into conversational traps that produced unwary answers. And if she didn't answer *that* question, he was quite capable of making his own assumptions. But he already had.

'It's what I said before, isn't it? Nigel wants that delectable face and figure of yours all to himself. He doesn't want to share it with the great buying public.'

'I can understand that——' Frankie began.

'As I told you, so can I.' A wickedly insinuative smile curled his large mouth and twinkled in his dark eyes. 'Especially after my privileged private view of a few moments ago.'

'Oh!' For an instant Frankie contemplated throwing the remainder of her meal at him. But it was too good to waste on this exasperating man.

'Don't even try it,' he said with that uncanny perception of his. 'I might be tempted to retaliate.'

At the thought of the pair of them, slinging fish and

chips at each other like a couple of warring school-children, Frankie's unpredictable sense of humour surfaced and a reluctant giggle escaped her.

'That's better,' Mike said with satisfaction. He poured an evilly strong-looking cup of tea and pushed it towards her.

Frankie peered into the cup, her nose wrinkling doubtfully. 'What did you use? Boot polish?'

'Go on!' he scoffed. 'There's nothing like a good cup of tea with fish and chips. None of your milk and hot water brews. That's something your aunt and I had in common. She couldn't abide what she called "gnat's pee" either.'

Whether it was his earthy humour, the fact that both she and the kitchen were warm, or that her stomach was comfortably full, or a combination of all three, Frankie wasn't sure. But she *was* aware of a euphoria she hadn't known in days.

In the flickering firelight the old kitchen looked less dreary and more homelike; and she suddenly felt she had known Mike for years, instead of a matter of days.

'Thanks for the supper, Mike,' she said with belated gratitude.

'My pleasure.' Aware of her softened mood, his eyes met hers and he reached across the table. 'Maybe it's time we called a truce,' he said. 'I know you resent the fact that your aunt made me her trustee. But, aside from that, there's no real reason why we shouldn't at least be civil to each other.'

She looked at him doubtfully. Their continual warring did all seem rather petty. Slowly she extended her hand. 'OK. Truce!' she confirmed.

But he did not immediately release her. Instead his grasp tightened. 'Frankie,' he said, 'if you weren't engaged to this Nigel would you be more likely to consider——?'

'Mike!' Prickly with awareness she snatched her hand free. 'Don't spoil things,' she told him. 'Don't start another row, please. Perhaps,' she added, 'it's time you went.' And, to lighten an atmosphere that to her seemed suddenly fraught with tension, 'Or you'll be putting in a bill for overtime.'

He took his dismissal without protest. But as she locked the door behind him, bolting and barring it this time, Frankie was not reassured. There had been something in the way he had held on to her hand, something in his expression, a note in his voice that she'd found profoundly disturbing.

She was imagining things, of course. After all, he'd made his disapproval of her pretty plain these last few days. But in future perhaps it would be as well if there were no more late-night encounters and definitely no more suppers à deux.

As her veterinary consultant, even as a friend, Mike was quite acceptable, but he meant no more to her than that. The sooner her fiancé put in an appearance, the better. It seemed necessary all of a sudden to remind herself that, even though she was not yet wearing Nigel's ring, their relationship was a serious commitment.

CHAPTER FOUR

FRANKIE had forgotten what fun decorating could be. The décor of her rented flat had been chosen by her landlady. But when Frankie's mother had been alive they had wallpapered and painted together. Of course, she assured herself, *this* job was only a matter of expediency—to brighten her *temporary* surroundings—but nevertheless it was extremely satisfying to stroke on the thick creamy paint and see the old kitchen taking on new life and light.

Dressed in jeans and sweater, protected by her aunt's old overall and a scarf tied about her fiery hair, Frankie's appearance was a far cry from that of the photographic model her friends and her fiancé knew. In fact she was very glad Nigel could not see her like this. He liked her to look glamorous.

So she wobbled dangerously on the rickety old ladder when a loud knock startled her. Goodness, suppose this *was* Nigel, at last. Unceremoniously dumping paintpot and brush, she scrambled down and ran to answer the door. She flung it open. Then stepped back.

'*You*!' she said accusingly.

'Me!' Mike agreed unrepentantly. 'Why? Who were you expecting? Patrick Lichfield? Lord Snowdon?'

Frankie quelled a snigger at the thought of either famous photographer catching her in this get-up. 'Well, not you, certainly,' she retorted. '*You* never knock. *You* just walk in.'

'Ah, but this is the new me.' Nevertheless he was across the threshold without waiting for an invitation. 'After last night I thought it might be more than my life was worth to walk in on you again.' And, as Frankie blushed at the recollection of last night, he regarded her paint-spattered clothes with interest. 'Is this some new fashion? Where are the cameras?' He peered about the kitchen in mock horror.

Frankie chuckled aloud this time, liking his sense of humour. Nigel would not have found her appearance at all amusing. He. . . But she caught herself back from the edge of disloyalty.

'I know,' she said ruefully, but still smiling. 'I look awful. These old walls were really filthy. And most of it seems to have rubbed off on me.' Not only that, she thought, but with her hair dragged back, face bare of make-up, she must look an absolute sight. Then, puzzled by something about Mike's silence, she looked at him to find an arrested expression in the dark eyes.

Frankie recognised the expression for what it was. But she had never expected to see that particular look in Mike Leeming's eyes. It certainly hadn't been there when he'd walked in upon her bathing. So why now, when she was looking distinctly unglamorous? A sense of danger prickled her nerve-ends and she reacted strangely.

'You're enjoying seeing me like this,' she snapped accusingly, 'aren't you?'

'Yes,' he agreed and then, surprisingly, 'it's a vast

improvement.' He held out his hand, something glinting in his palm. 'I thought I'd better return the spare key. Your aunt gave it to me in case of emergencies. I doubt if anyone else, apart from the donkeys, would have noticed if she hadn't appeared one morning.'

But, to her own surprise, Frankie found herself shaking her head. 'You'd better keep it,' she told him. And, hastily, as he looked curiously at her, 'Not for my sake. But in case of something like yesterday happening and my not being here to see to the animals. And what are *you* grinning at?' she enquired indignantly.

'Nothing, nothing at all.' His rugged face was the picture of innocence.

'Oh, yes, you are. And I know what it is. You needn't think I'm getting attached to the wretched creatures. I still don't intend to bury myself here for the rest of my life.'

'No, of course not. There's no need for that.' Amazingly he agreed with her, making her look at him suspiciously. 'If you take on a couple of helpers, as I suggested, you'll have plenty of time for a social life too. The country has quite as many delights to offer as the city.'

Frankie parted her lips to remind him for the—but she wasn't sure how many times—that she wouldn't be staying to sample the local life. But something comically expectant about his expression made her laugh resignedly instead.

'You're incorrigible, Mike Leeming.' Then, 'Do you want a coffee? I'm about ready for one myself.'

He accepted with alacrity and, as she prepared it, he prowled about the kitchen, inspecting the progress of her work. He picked up the paint can. 'It *is* non-drip,' he observed to no one in particular.

'All right! All right! I know!' Frankie said over her shoulder. 'I don't need you to tell me. I must be the only person in the world who can make non-drip paint do the opposite.'

'I'd lend you a hand,' Mike told her, 'but I've still got my calls to make. I don't suppose,' he said with unusual hesitance for him, 'that you feel like a break from all this?' He indicated the half-finished kitchen.

Frankie looked at him questioningly.

'I *was* wondering if you felt like coming out on my rounds with me? You haven't seen any of the surrounding countryside yet. I know it's not at its best in January but——'

'But you'd like me to get an idea of what it has to offer,' Frankie said, straight-faced.

'Right!' he agreed.

He didn't fool her for a moment, Frankie thought. He had merely changed his tactics, from aggression to persuasive charm. It would get him nowhere.

'Mike, you must be the most transparent person it's ever been my misfortune to know. I can see right through you.'

'Oh, no, you can't,' he contradicted. And suddenly the laughter was gone from his face. He came over to her and turned her away from her task. 'There's a lot about me you don't know yet, Frankie Latimer,' he told her, his dark eyes intent upon her suddenly flushed face. 'A lot that I'm not ready to tell you yet—and a lot more that you're not ready to hear.' He licked a finger and rubbed a paint spot from the tip of her nose.

Her breathing oddly constricted, Frankie stared back at him, caught in the snare of dark grey eyes, her own gaze troubled, searching for the same unbidden response in the rugged face. But he revealed nothing, whereas she. . . As always she was far too conscious of him, she realised, his proximity, the sheer masculine bulk of him. She thought she could identify his every separate aroma—his tangy aftershave, the crisp cleanliness of his clothes and a warm indefinable something that was totally male, totally compelling. An animal magnetism that transcended the rugged features. Mike in a friendly mood posed too much of a threat to her composure. She thought that she almost preferred it when they were at odds with each other.

He must be aware of her tension, she realised, and hastily she broke away from the large hands pressed down on her shoulders. 'Your. . .your coffee's ready,' she told him. It seemed to be difficult to get the words out.

To her relief he accepted the mug from her slightly tremulous fingers and moved across the kitchen. He was once again just Mike, ordinary, unthreatening. But even so it took Frankie some time to regain her composure. Why—in spite of everything—did she find him so attractive, experience this incandescent physical response to his touch, his slightest proximity? He just wasn't her type.

'So, how about it?'

She stared at him blankly.

'My rounds? The guided tour?'

What had she thought he meant? She really must be more careful about letting her ridiculous imaginings intrude upon reality. But she found that she wanted to go with him. And yet. . . And yet she knew it might be wiser to refuse. She sought for a convincing excuse. 'I ought to finish the painting.'

He swept the excuse aside. 'There's far too much to finish in one day. You'll only make yourself overtired and then you'll be in no fit state to cope with the evening chores.'

'Putting the donkeys' welfare first again,' she taunted. But he did not rise.

'Come on!' he coaxed.

Their route took them through Lionswick village.

'My place,' Mike indicated with a casual wave of one large hand as they passed the entrance to his drive.

Frankie did not reveal that she already knew where he lived, that she would have dearly liked to see inside his house. She didn't want him to get the idea that she took any undue interest in his private life. For instance, did he have a girlfriend? He'd said he wasn't married, but surely he hadn't reached his age—late thirties, early forties?—and remained entirely celibate.

What was that you said about not taking an undue interest in him? she chided herself and resolutely dragged her attention back to what he was saying, as they left the village behind and drove out into the surrounding lanes.

'This is one of the few areas of the Cotswolds that doesn't get overrun with tourists. And personally I hope it stays that way. In other places a lot of what we call incomers have bought up property and brought a whole new way of life with them.'

The Land Rover slowed and pulled to a stop in a gateway. They were miles from anywhere and Frankie glanced nervously at Mike. But it seemed he had no intentions to which she could possibly object.

Anyone would think you wished he *had*, she told herself crossly, as something almost akin to disappointment stabbed through her, when it seemed all he had in mind was a lecture on the beauty of their surroundings.

'Just try and imagine this lane in spring and summer,' he told her. 'Birds in full throat, the air thick with pollen, the fields bright with yellow rape.' The earnest timbre of his deep voice conveyed his very real love of the countryside. 'Try and imagine the pungent smell of the cow parsley. Just picture rabbits careering back and forth across the road, almost under our wheels. What has London to offer that's comparable with that?'

Because of his obvious sincerity, Frankie answered him without rancour. 'Mike, I'm not denying that the countryside is a beautiful place—for visits and holidays. But——'

'And it's a beautiful place to live. When you're weighing up the pros and cons of the future, Frankie, just put some of the things I've mentioned into the balance.'

He drove on and, while Frankie tried to discount what he had said, its effect upon her, she found herself looking with new eyes at her surroundings, remembering wistfully the child she had been, who *had* loved the countryside, who had once said to her aunt—and she had forgotten that until this moment—'I wish *I* lived here, Auntie Francesca.'

Mike had about half a dozen calls to make. Frankie would have been quite content to remain in the Land Rover. But at each property they visited he insisted on her accompanying him.

'I'd like you to meet some of the people round here, honest, sincere country folk.' He made it sound, Frankie thought, as though townsfolk were the complete opposite. She was quite convinced that this outing was another of his ploys to convert her to his way of thinking. 'One or two of them are real "characters",' Mike went on, 'men of the soil, who've rarely been outside the county all their lives. But unfortunately they're a dying breed.'

One of their stops was at a smallholding, just an isolated cottage and a couple of fields.

'Jed Spriggs, the old boy who lives here, has to go into hospital soon,' Mike told Frankie as they made their way round to the rear door. 'And it's unlikely he'll be fit to live here afterwards. He's asked me to try and find good temporary homes for his livestock. But I think he knows, in his heart of hearts, that they'll have to be permanent homes.'

Frankie stopped in her tracks. 'He hasn't got any donkeys, has he?' she demanded suspiciously.

'Frankie!' Mike sounded wounded, but there was laughter beneath the outrage. 'Do you really think I'm as devious as that?'

'Yes,' she said uncompromisingly.

But he was not a bit offended. Instead he gave a great shout of laughter and flung an arm about her shoulders, hugging her to him, arousing a leaping response that she feared might be discernible to him.

'You're getting to know me,' he said with awful complacency. As if that must be her overriding desire in life, Frankie thought exasperatedly as she side-stepped out of his clasp. In one sense she was glad they were not continually at each other's throats now. But it cleared the way for other emotions. She was, she knew, in danger of liking Mike Leeming rather a lot. And that was out of the question. 'And no,' he assured her, 'there are no donkeys.'

'So what *are* you up to?' she asked, determined not to move another step until he'd told her. But he was not to be drawn.

'Come and see for yourself.' He took hold of her hand and tugged her onwards. Frankie knew she ought not to permit his clasp. But, she excused her weak submission, they were crossing badly rutted ground and she didn't want to risk twisting an ankle.

The stock, which privately Frankie considered to be a pitiful living for the incredibly ancient man who greeted them, consisted of a few geese and a couple of cows in calf. The ancient seemed pathetically grateful for their visit and admitted to having known Frankie's aunt.

'Though not in the Biblical sense,' Mike whispered wickedly in her ear, so that she had to bite hard on her quivering lips. She couldn't recall Nigel having ever made her want to laugh like this. It seemed like treachery to enjoy Mike's company so much.

'A real lady, that's what *she* were,' Jed Spriggs declared. 'I wouldn't have minded too much old Daisy and Blossom going to her place. And I reckon you've a lot of her about you. So it's very grateful I am.'

'Just think,' Mike told her enthusiastically and before she could get a word in, 'how useful the milk will be, for mixing with the donkeys' feed. As it is, the milk bill at your place is astronomical. It will be an economy in the long run for you to have your own cows.'

'There's no way——' Frankie began determinedly, then caught sight of the old man's eager face and remembered where he was going and what might happen. 'Honestly, Mike,' she muttered, 'I could kick you. You'd no right to build up his hopes before consulting me. And you *did*, didn't you?' she accused.

He was unrepentant. 'Only because I've found out that basically you're kind-hearted—if a little misguided.'

'Misguided?' What on earth was he talking about? He didn't leave her in doubt for long.

'Misguided in thinking you want to be a beautiful porcelain doll all your life and,' he added wickedly, 'marry a townee called Nigel.'

And yet somehow, despite her outrage, before they drove away from the smallholding it had been agreed that Mike would make arrangements for Daisy and Blossom to be picked up and transported to the Donkey Sanctuary at Lionswick.

'Thanks, love!' Disconcertingly, as they got back in the Land Rover Mike leaned over and dropped a light kiss on her cheek. 'Those animals mean a lot to the old boy.'

It was ridiculous just how much that fleeting kiss, so lightly bestowed, disturbed her. It hadn't meant anything, of course, she thought, trying to quell the sudden singing in her blood. Quite probably he was accustomed to saluting her aunt in the same way. If he'd been as fond of her as he claimed, he had probably looked upon her as he would one of his own elderly relatives. The difference was that Frankie was *not* elderly and he had no right to kiss her, however casually. And she tried to speak as if it had not happened.

'I don't mind the cows. But I'm *not* having the geese,' she said as severely as she could manage. 'I always have been and I always will be terrified of geese. Sneaky, hissing things.' Then, her nerves settling a little as they set off on the remainder of the round, 'I hope,' she said sarcastically, 'that no more of your calls involve animals requiring foster homes?'

He was able to assure her, truthfully, she discovered to her relief, that they did not.

They were back at the old farmhouse in plenty of time for evening chores and Mike insisted on helping. To Frankie it seemed inconsistent behaviour for a man who had been so anxious to jettison just such responsibilities.

'Won't your mother be expecting you? For a meal or something?' she asked as they stood at the kitchen table, stirring up the mix. He had confessed that one of the advantages of having his mother stay with him was that of regularly prepared meals.

'She's expecting both of us,' he confounded Frankie by saying.

She stopped stirring to look at him. 'Both of us? You're joking?'

'No,' he assured her. 'And don't argue for once. It's

all fixed and she'll be very annoyed if I come back without you.'

'You have the cheek of the devil,' Frankie exclaimed. And then, on a totally unexpected wave of euphoria, 'Give me one good reason why I should save you from her displeasure,' she teased.

'Because, in spite of your determinedly prickly manner, you're beginning to like me,' he said with infuriating certainty. 'And you wouldn't like to see a pal hung, drawn and quartered.'

Frankie fought valiantly and succeeded—just—in hiding a smile. 'I wouldn't blame your mother a bit if she developed homicidal tendencies, living with you,' she told him. 'You're the most aggravating man *I* know.'

'Doesn't Nigel ever aggravate you?' he wanted to know.

'No,' she said firmly and not altogether truthfully. The mention of Nigel sobered her. Somehow she didn't want to talk about him. And to her relief Mike did not press the subject.

'So will you come to dinner?'

Frankie had a great deal of self-sufficiency about her character and she had never been afraid of her own company. But after the past few days of solitary exist-ence it *would* be nice to have a change.

'All right,' she conceded. 'Though not for your sake, but for your mother's. You've obviously put her to a great deal of trouble.'

'Not a bit. It was her idea. She's very anxious to meet you.'

'Why should she want to meet *me*?'

'Oh,' Mike stared innocently at the kitchen ceiling, 'she's always been very particular about my friends—ever since I was a child.'

Because of his initial hostility towards her, it gave Frankie a warm feeling to hear herself described as a friend, but she hid her reaction under a retaliatory taunt. '*Another* mummy's boy!'

Then she could have bitten out her tongue at his triumphant, 'Ah-hah! So Nigel *is* a mummy's boy.'

'I didn't say *that*,' she denied hotly.

'No.' And then, hastily, as she glared at him, 'All right, *pax*. But I was serious about my mother being keen to meet you.' He waited expectantly but this time Frankie decided not to ask why. In truth she was a little afraid of the answer.

Instead, she asked, 'She doesn't "dress" for dinner, does she? Because I'm afraid I haven't——'

'Just a wash and brush up will do,' he assured her. 'Doting mother that she is, she won't let even *me* sit down smelling of the farmyard.'

Frankie was still laughing as she went upstairs to comply. In Mike's company she seemed to swing between laughter and exasperation and yet, she discovered, it was a good feeling. Suddenly she was looking forward to seeing his home and—though with some trepidation—to meeting his mother. *Would* she be another Mrs Greaves?

Mike's home was built of the golden stone Frankie had by now come to recognise as typical of her surroundings. It was square and solid but not as large as she had expected. The surgery, he explained, was housed in a separate block around the back, together with a range of outbuildings used for any animal that needed to be kept under observation.

The first thing that struck Frankie about Mike's house was the all-enveloping warmth, a strong contrast to her present abode. No lack of central heating here. But there was more than artificial warmth in her welcome as Mrs Leeming came out into the hall to greet them.

'So you managed to persuade her. I told you charm would work better than your usual bossy tactics. Hello, my dear. Mike tells me you prefer to be known as Frankie, though Francesca is a lovely name.'

'I use it professionally,' Frankie admitted, 'but it's a bit of a mouthful for private use.' She liked the look of Mike's mother. There was nothing to remind her of Mrs Greaves's dauntingly cold manner. Like Mike, his mother was tall, and she had the same expressive dark eyes and heavy eyebrows. But whereas his hair was black, except for a few distinguished grey hairs at the temples, his mother's was snow-white.

'Dinner's almost ready,' Mrs Leeming said. To Frankie she added, 'I usually take the time Mike tells me and add half an hour.'

'Why,' Frankie asked with a mischievous glance at him, 'is he so unreliable?'

'Off with you, Mike,' his mother ordered, 'and get cleaned up.'

'So that you two can take the opportunity to tear my character to shreds,' he grumbled, but nevertheless he headed off up the stairs.

'Actually,' Mrs Leeming confided as she led Frankie

into the main living-room, 'he's *very* reliable in most things. I couldn't have wished for a better son. But where his work's concerned. . .' She shrugged. 'His father was just the same.'

'Was he a vet too?'

'Yes, dear. This was originally his practice. I was so glad when Mike decided to follow in Jim's footsteps. He took over when Jim retired and thank goodness Jim lived to see him just as popular as ever *he* was.' All of this was said without a trace of the maudlin emotion Mrs Greaves would have employed in speaking of *her* late husband.

They sat down. Frankie was dying to look about her and get some idea of Mike's lifestyle, but that had to be postponed, for Mrs Leeming was regarding her intently and Frankie had perforce to return her gaze.

'Yes, dear.' The older woman nodded. 'Mike's right. You *do* have a look of your aunt. Though I only met her once or twice. And of course you're young and pretty. I can quite see why. . .' She broke off and went on in a different vein, 'And how are you settling in at the sanctuary? Everyone calls it that, though I believe the place is really Lionswick Farm.'

Although Frankie would have strenuously denied that she was 'settling in', she found herself relating for her hostess's benefit the details of the past few days and in doing so made an amusing story of its trials and tribulations.

Mrs Leeming was nodding again—with approval this time. 'It sounds as if you're fitting in very nicely, dear. An ability to see the comical side of things is such a help in life, isn't it? Thank heaven my dear husband

and I shared the same sense of humour. So important in a marriage, I always think. And I'm glad to say Mike has inherited it. No wonder you and he get along so splendidly.'

By this time Frankie was fidgeting uncomfortably. It did not sound as if Mrs Leeming knew about the early antagonistic days of her acquaintance with Mike. So what, she wondered, had he been saying about her?

'Mrs Leeming,' she began, 'Mike and I——'

'I thought the pair of you would find plenty to talk about.' Mike had not taken very long over his ablutions. Now he strode across the room and stood with his back to the fire—a real one, despite the efficient central heating. He had changed into impeccably tailored trousers, the muscles in his long legs outlined by their snug fit, and a shirt of some soft silky material which moulded itself to his broad chest. Until this evening Frankie had never seen him in anything but his rather disreputable working clothes. But it struck her that it did not seem to matter what he wore. It was the man, not the clothes. And before she could prevent it the disloyal thought had crept insidiously into her mind that Mike was so much more of a man than Nigel. Nigel hated to get dirty and untidy. Mike didn't seem to care about that—and yet it did not disgust her.

'Do I have any reputation left?' Mike was enquiring.

'What on earth makes you think we'd want to talk about *you*?' Frankie demanded before his mother could answer him. 'There are far more interesting topics.'

Mother and son laughed together, exchanging affectionate glances. His said, I told you so, while hers was approving, its complacency ridiculously like Mike at his most smug. Just you wait until I get you on your own, Mike Leeming, Frankie thought. I'll find out exactly what you've been saying about me. And then. . . And then what? She found she did not at all know how to deal with Mike Leeming, nor how to deal with the very unsettling thoughts she was beginning to have about him. The sooner she decided what she was going to do about the sanctuary and went back to London—and Nigel—the better.

The way she felt about Nigel was *safe*. It did not pose any threat to her self-containment. From what she had witnessed of her parents' marriage, Frankie was convinced that it was a mistake for a woman to be totally enslaved by her emotions.

But despite her reservations about Mike's company, she had to admit to enjoying a very pleasant evening. It was a real treat not to have to cook for herself, and Mike and his mother proved to be two of the most entertaining people she had met in a long time. Mrs Leeming had spoken the truth when she'd said they shared a sense of humour, and between them they tossed the conversational ball lightly back and forth, keeping Frankie in a constant state of helpless laughter.

So that she was amazed and not a little disappointed when she realised the evening was over and Mike was ready to take her home. Home! She examined the word. It was the first time she had thought of Lionswick Farm in that way. But it was just a convenient term having no significance, she told herself.

Mrs Leeming waved aside her genuine thanks. 'It was a pleasure to meet you, my dear. And I hope you'll come again soon. You mustn't become a recluse, like your aunt, however much you enjoy being with those old donkeys.'

Mike's hastily stifled guffaw made Frankie want to kick him and she assured Mrs Leeming with greater earnestness than necessary that she had absolutely no intention of becoming tied to the sanctuary.

'She liked you,' Mike said as they drove back along the narrow lanes to the farm.

'*I* liked *her*,' Frankie was able to say with truth. 'But, Mike, what have you been——?'

'Better than Nigel's mother?' he asked.

There was no doubt in Frankie's mind that she infinitely preferred the jolly Mrs Leeming to Nigel's carping, disapproving mother, but loyalty forbade her to admit it, so she remained silent—for all the good it did her.

'I shall take your silence for assent,' Mike told her.

'I've always found comparisons odious,' she retorted crossly.

'So you won't have compared Nigel with me.'

The guilty knowledge that she had in fact begun to do so made Frankie sharp. 'No!' she snapped.

'Why? Which of us did you fear might suffer from the comparison?'

'Neither of you. You're. . .you're totally different. Comparisons just aren't possible.'

'Oh, dear! Oh, dear!' He sighed exaggeratedly.

'What do you mean, "oh, dear"?' she demanded.

'I mean that if Nigel is *so* different from me, he's definitely not the right man for *you*.'

'Well! Really!' Frankie gasped.

He took up the word but in a different context. 'Yes,

really. *You* need someone you can laugh with and yet rely on.'

'Nigel and I *do* laugh at things. And I *can* rely on him. That's one of the most important things about him. He's solid and reliable.'

'But you can't rely on him to visit you here, it seems? You haven't even heard from him.'

'Mike!' she exclaimed, with all of the usual exasperation he was capable of arousing in her. 'Stop it! Stop knocking Nigel. You've never met him. You don't know what he's like. I *do* know him. I *love* him. I'm going to marry him. And I won't listen to any more of your insinuations. You're just trying to cause trouble because you want me to take over the sanctuary. Well, even if Nigel didn't exist, I wouldn't do that. Drop me here, please. I'll walk the rest of the way.' And, as the Land Rover showed no signs of slowing, 'I said *stop*, Mike!'

This time he complied, so suddenly that Frankie was thrown off balance. Before she could regain her equilibrium and scramble out, two large hands took her by the shoulders—a favourite gesture of his—and turned her towards him.

In the dark interior of the cab she could not see his face but she could sense that it was not far from her own. At once she was aware of that suffocating sexual attraction he exuded, the attraction she had been resisting almost from the moment of their first meeting.

'All right, Frankie,' he said quietly, very quietly. 'I'll stop insulting your beloved Nigel. Obviously you've got to find out the truth for yourself—the truth about *yourself* as much as anything else. But,' and now there was a note of wicked mischief in his voice, 'I do think you're doing yourself a disservice, refusing to make comparisons. How about comparing *this* for a start?'

She knew what he was going to do, but a suffocating blankness in her brain prevented speech or movement.

His mouth covered hers, not in a brief kiss, but for a long, long time and with a devastating seriousness that she felt in every fibre of her being. She fought desperately against the response that she felt welling up inside her, but, as the kiss went on and on, her blood began to pound deafeningly in her ears and it became impossible to breathe, as impossible as it was to disguise the effect he was having on her.

Though her mind might still scream resistance, her body seemed to have a will of its own, responding with primitive ardour to his maleness.

Besides, he was so strong that there was no way she could break free of him and she knew the kiss would continue until *he* was ready to end it.

'Well, Frankie,' when he finally released her his breathing sounded a little ragged, but nothing like as disturbed as hers felt, 'how did *that* compare with one of Nigel's kisses?'

She took a deep gulp of air, struggled for composure, succeeded. 'I wouldn't be so cruel as to hurt your feelings,' she told him.

'Why, you little liar!' She thought he sounded angry but then he gave a short bark, which was a laugh nevertheless, before he started up the Land Rover again and drove on.

'I said I'd walk from here,' Frankie protested, though she was not sure her legs would be capable of carrying her. They felt oddly weak and shaky. Dear lord! *Had* she ever felt like that when Nigel had kissed her? Her confused brain could not remember any such previous experience.

'If you think I'm leaving you in this dark, lonely lane, to be attacked by some lunatic——'

'I thought I already had been.'

There was silence for a moment. Then Mike laughed. 'If you think *that* was insanity,' he said lightly, 'how about this? How about marrying *me*, instead of Nigel? That way you could stay on here and run the sanctuary, the way your aunt wanted you to.'

CHAPTER FIVE

FRANKIE'S first reaction was one of stunned disbelief. Mike *couldn't* have said what she *thought* he'd said. But then he angled her a brief glance and she knew that her ears had not deceived her.

'What, no comment?' he mocked. 'First time I've ever known *you* at a loss for words.'

Frankie pulled herself together 'I didn't think such a ridiculous remark warranted a reply,' she told him.

'Oh?' he enquired tautly.

'No.' Frankie regained her usual fluency. 'If I believed for one moment it was a serious remark, I'd tell you exactly what I thought of it—and you. As it is, I think you have a pretty poor taste in jokes.'

'I see.' As they jolted over the rutted drive up to the farmhouse, he was silent, a silence which Frankie began to find uncomfortable. Then, as he pulled up by the back door, 'You're right, of course, it *was* a poor joke.'

He said no more but sat there, obviously waiting for her to get out. But for a moment Frankie did not move. Somehow what had been an enjoyable afternoon and evening had suddenly gone flat. She felt. . .yes, she felt as though she were the one in the wrong, whereas it had been Mike who had spoiled everything by his tasteless humour. There was no reason on earth why *she* should apologise to *him*. And yet. . .

'Mike——' she began.

'Well, goodnight, Frankie,' he interrupted before she could get any further.

There was nothing she could do except comply with his hint. She opened the door and slid down from the Land Rover's high seat.

'Please thank your mother again for me,' she said formally. 'And. . .and thank *you*.'

'For what?' he enquired sarcastically. He reached over and slammed the passenger door shut. The engine was still running and now he accelerated away, making a wide sweep of the yard, not looking back, without any gesture of farewell. And Frankie let herself into the house, feeling unaccountably depressed—and guilty.

He couldn't possibly have been serious about his unconventional proposal—could he? No, of course not. Why, he'd even made a joke of it. So why had he been so furious when *she* had treated it as such?

Oh! Frankie sighed exasperatedly. Mike wasn't *worth* these twinges of conscience, she told herself sternly as she got ready for bed. He was detestable, a man who swung between aggression and false charm to obtain his own ends. Whether he was bullying her or pressing his unwanted kisses upon her, he had not treated her as she believed a man *should* treat a woman.

He was a rough, uncouth countryman, she tried to persuade herself, whereas Nigel was smooth, self-possessed, innately courteous to all women. Her relationship with Nigel did not depend on violent, shattering sexuality. Mike was a boor! And she hated him. Which was no good reason for Frankie lying

awake well into the small hours with a feeling similar
to that of having murdered her best friend.

It was a tired Frankie, decidedly out of sorts with
herself, who carried out the stable chores next morning.
And by the time she had groomed the twentieth donkey
she had come to a decision. Mike was right about one
thing. She *didn't* have to go on coping by herself. In
fact the sooner she roped in some suitable help, the
sooner she could get back to London and to a civilised
way of life. And away from Mike? She brushed that
thought aside. Somehow it didn't bear too close an
investigation.

Mike had spoken of the possibility of hiring local
teenagers. And she supposed he would know of suitable youngsters. But after last night there was no way
she was going to contact him.

She changed out of her working clothes and went
down to the village, to put a postcard advertisement in
the window of the post-office-cum-hardware-store. The
postmistress was encouraging, sure that Frankie would
soon be inundated with offers.

Back at the house once more she decided to try and
telephone Nigel. Today was normally his day off, a day
he invariably spent on one of his DIY projects, or on
the large garden.

Her heart sank when Mrs Greaves answered.

'No, he's not here.'

'He's not *still* in Scotland?'

'No. He's gone abroad.'

'Abroad?' Information from Mrs Greaves was always
obtained in small grudging doses.

'To a book fair.'

'Did he see my letter before he went?'

'Letter? He's had no letter.'

The lying old bat, Frankie fulminated. Of course Mrs Greaves would have recognised her handwriting and contrived to 'lose' it. She had to face it, there was simply no way she was going to get at Nigel via his mother. She would just have to wait until she could contact him directly. Or, a new thought struck her, by leaving a message with his employers. He would have to go into the office when he returned to England.

'Thanks,' she said shortly and—under her breath—'for nothing.' She replaced the receiver then dialled the publisher's number. A helpful secretary confirmed that Nigel was still abroad.

Her failure to contact Nigel made her even more determined to get matters sorted out here and get back to London. Besides which she must contact her agent to see if he had any modelling jobs lined up for her. As Mike had tactlessly pointed out, there were plenty of girls ready and willing to step into her shoes if she disappeared from the scene.

'Not at the moment, love,' was the discouraging response. 'Not much call for redheads right now. They all seem to be into blondes. But keep in touch.' It was almost as if Mike had *wished* this situation on her, Frankie brooded.

The telephone rang just after lunch and she sprang to answer it. Perhaps, just for once, one of her messages had got through to her fiancé. But although it was a familiar voice that spoke her name it was not Nigel.

'Frankie?' Mike said and her heart gave a little

unexpected bump and a wave of relief swept over her. So he was still speaking to her.

'Yes?' She tried to keep the eagerness out of her voice.

'I've just seen your postcard in the post office window.'

'Yes.' Lightly, 'So you see I do sometimes take your advice.'

'I wouldn't have advised you to go about it in *that* way. It's not a very sensible way of advertising for reliable help,' he said, his criticism immediately quelling her little surge of spirits. If that was the only reason he'd telephoned her. . . 'Why didn't you ask *me* to help you find someone?' And as Frankie did not immediately answer, 'Oh, all right, I suppose I can guess the answer to that one. But you should be more careful. There are undesirable elements in village life, you know, just as much as in a city. If anyone applies, let me know, will you? I'd like to be there when you interview them.'

'I don't think that will be necessary,' Frankie told him coolly. 'I think I'm a fairly good judge of character.'

'I see.' He sounded grim. 'So it's back to square one, is it? Just because of a. . .a humorous suggestion. It seems I shall have to revise my opinion of *you*—yet again—and just as I thought I'd got you neatly pigeon-holed.'

'And what's that supposed to mean?' Frankie demanded.

'You wouldn't be interested in *my* opinion of you.'

'Maybe not. But it's never stopped you giving it before.'

'*That* was only a brief résumé. I *could* go into the subject at some length. But I don't have the time to spare just now.' And before Frankie could draw breath for an angry retort, 'I'm off up to Jed Spriggs's place. The hospital have sent for him. I'll be round to your place later with Daisy and Blossom.' And he rang off, fortunately before Frankie could be tempted into the childish retaliation of telling him what he could do with Jed's cows.

Instead, she vented her spleen on the kitchen walls, splashing on the paint with vicious slaps of the brush, rehearsing meanwhile some of the things she would like to say to Mike Leeming.

As always with such internal dialogues, she reached the state where she could almost believe that the imagined conversation had actually taken place so that, when she heard a cattle truck rumbling into the yard later that afternoon, she was well primed for trouble.

Paintbrush still in hand, she threw open the back door in time to see the back of the truck let down, releasing the two cows and. . .a gaggle of geese, their sinuous necks waving this way and that as they inspected these new surroundings.

'Hey!' she shouted. She strode across the yard, an avenging fury going to war armed with an uplifted brush. She glared into the dark recesses of the truck. 'You lying, scheming. . .!' she addressed the dimly seen figure. 'I *told* you not to bring the geese. I won't *have* them here. So you can just load them up again and——'

'Nothing to do with me, miss.' The man who straightened up and came towards her was a total stranger. 'Just acting on Mr Leeming's orders.'

If Frankie had been annoyed before, she was even more furious now. She had been made to look foolish in front of this unknown man—and Mike Leeming was to blame.

'Where *is* Mr Leeming?' she demanded. '*He* was supposed to——'

'Called out to an emergency. He asked me to stand in for him.' The man held out his hand. 'I'm Bill Hardy, old Jed's nearest neighbour.'

'Couldn't *you* have taken the geese, then?' Frankie asked, casting the still investigating birds a look of loathing.

'Sorry, miss.' He grinned. 'Be more than my life's worth. My wife's like you. Can't stand 'em.'

It would be more than Mike Leeming's life was worth too when she got hold of him, Frankie seethed. What a nerve, dumping the geese on her like this and after she'd made it a specific condition. Oh, just wait till she could confront him. But it was her own fault, of course. She shouldn't have weakened over the cows. She'd given him an inch and he'd taken the proverbial yard.

'Where d'you want the beasts?' Bill Hardy was waiting patiently for her instructions.

'The barn's ready for them. I'll show you.' She was very relieved that Bill had not just abandoned his charges. She had no experience of herding cows. And here, without Mike's reassuring bulk, Daisy and Blossom looked much larger.

'The old girls will need milking right away,' Bill said. 'Know how, do you?'

'Yes,' Frankie was glad to be able to say. So far Bill Hardy must have a very bad impression of her. And milking a cow couldn't be very different from milking a goat. It had been a long time ago, of course. But surely, like riding a bicycle, you didn't forget how.

As soon as Bill Hardy had driven away, she went back into the house to fetch the new buckets she'd bought that morning at the village hardware store. With these and an old three-legged stool found in a corner of the barn, Frankie felt equipped for her task—and not a little smug that this was something she could manage without Mike's supervision.

Half an hour later the buckets were still empty. Daisy and Blossom were complaining lustily and Frankie was on the verge of tears. The cows were making so much noise that she did not hear the approaching vehicle and the first she knew of Mike's arrival was his exasperated comment.

'I thought you said you knew how to milk.' And she was lifted bodily aside.

Mike took her place with his dark head leaning against Daisy's heaving flanks. And soon the rhythmic movement of his large hands had the creamy liquid gushing into the first of the pails.

Fascinated by his expertise, Frankie watched, until she found herself conjuring up other and more disturbing images of uses to which he might put those coaxing hands, images she firmly suppressed and, by the time he had also dealt with Blossom, she had regained her composure and was ready to face him with a tirade instead of tears.

'Don't you dare say a word,' she warned him as he turned to look quizzically at her. '*You* wished those animals on to me. And I agreed—for that old man's sake. But I told you before, I've changed. I'm *not* one of your country bumpkins. I've forgotten all I ever knew about milking and I——'

'No, you haven't,' Mike interrupted. His tone was soothing. He stood up and, before she could evade his touch, he took hold of her and pushed her down on to the stool he had vacated. Its seat still radiated *his* warmth and Frankie felt a shock that was almost electric run through her. 'You haven't forgotten,' he repeated. 'But you and the animals are strangers to each other. You have to gain their confidence. Relax and they'll be relaxed. You allowed yourself to get all tensed up. Now——' he guided her '—put your hands here, and here, like so.' He demonstrated the action for her, made her repeat it as Blossom obligingly gave up a few more drops of milk. '*You see*! Like falling off a log.'

He pulled her to her feet again, looking down at her with a smile of tolerant amusement. With one hand he lifted her chin and looked down into her still-mutinous face. 'Don't scowl like that. You'll spoil your beauty.' With the finger of his free hand he smoothed away the frown lines from between her eyes.

It was a pleasant sensation, too pleasant when combined with the primitive spell of his masculinity and Frankie, realising the effect it was having upon her, jerked away.

'Much you'd care about that!' she jeered. 'Nothing would please you more than to see me become a wrinkled old hag.'

He recaptured her, holding her shoulders, giving her a little admonitory shake. 'Now, now, that's temper speaking. It just isn't so. I would hate to see the destruction of such loveliness. I'm as susceptible to female beauty as the next man and *you* are *very* beautiful.' His voice was a little husky. 'Too beautiful for comfort sometimes.'

His grasp tightened and Frankie wasn't sure if he realised he had pulled her a little closer. What she was sure of was that his closeness was affecting her in a very peculiar way. To her nostrils there came the faint, teasing aroma of male and she had the sudden desire to rest against Mike's strength, to feel his arms go around her, hold her, protect her. In fact, if he had not been grasping her so firmly, she might actually have swayed towards him.

Her eyes, drawn to his, seemed incapable of looking away and Frankie drew a little shuddering breath. Something strange was happening to her and she didn't want it. How was it possible that this man could move her so much, just by his simplest touch? He didn't even need to kiss her to have her bemused by waves of sheer sensuality. Dimly she realised he was still speaking.

'You have the same bone-structure as your aunt.' His finger was tracing her face as he spoke, the high cheekbones, the line of her jaw. And the muscles in Frankie's throat moved nervously as she swallowed. 'Even in her eighties,' Mike went on, 'even with her skin weather-beaten and lined, old Francesca was still beautiful and you will be too, if you don't allow life to spoil the inner you. Frankie!'

His hand was back at her chin now, lifting her face so that it was tilted up to his, and without her being aware of any movement on either part their bodies were touching now. The odd sensation in the pit of her stomach intensified, and she was embarrassingly aware that her breasts had tautened, thankful for the thick sweater that concealed them.

'Frankie, don't let that glossy world you've inhabited of late spoil you. Don't let yourself become one of these hard, vain women with no thoughts beyond their appearance and the admiration of men unworthy of you.'

His lowered head was so close now that Frankie could feel his breath softly upon her lips. It would take such a small movement for his mouth to close over hers and for a moment she wanted that, wanted it with such a ferocity that *she* might have initiated that move. But Mike went on.

'Has your Nigel ever seen you like this, I wonder? Untidy, flushed with exertion and infinitely more beautiful and desirable than——'

'Mike, stop it!'

She wrenched free of him. The mention of Nigel had been all that was needed to bring her to her senses. What on earth had she been about, allowing this man to hold her in his arms, to reach the point where she was actually about to invite his kiss? And it would have come to that. Frankie had no doubts at all about that. And that would have been very different from having his kisses *forced* upon her.

But she had to crush this dangerous attraction she felt—now—before she did something she would forever be ashamed of. She, who had always prized loyalty above any other virtue. Besides, this cajolery, this exertion of his. . .his masculinity, was just another weapon in Mike's armoury and it wouldn't get him any further than the other ruses he had employed.

'Don't think,' she told him with deliberate coldness, 'that you're going to get round me by flattery. You've tried just about every other method of persuading me to——'

'Is that what you think this is all about?' His expression had changed, hardened.

'Well, of course. I may not be good at the practicalities of country life. But I'm not a complete idiot, Mike. Even before we met, you disapproved of me. And apart from the fact that we declared a truce nothing else has changed. I'm still the same person, with the same views, the same determination to live my life the way *I* want to live it. So don't think I'm going to be fooled by a little flirtation into doing what *you* want me to do.'

But Mike did not give up that easily. He picked up the pails, now brimming with milk. 'Come on, now, Frankie,' he coaxed. 'You've had a trying half-hour and it hasn't done your temper any good. That's understandable. But there's no need to take it out on me. What you need is a pick-me-up. Let's go and put the kettle on and discuss this rationally.'

But Frankie dared not let herself be soothed and placated. Antagonism was safer than the other more dangerous emotions Mike aroused in her.

'I thought,' she jeered with deliberate intent to annoy, 'that only old women saw a cup of tea as a sovereign remedy for everything. And don't try your tactics on me any more. You've gone too far this time.'

'And so have *you*,' he told her grimly. He put down the pails once more and blocked her way to the barn door. 'It might do for your precious Nigel, but *I'll* not stand for you accusing *me* of being an old woman. What would you have me do, Frankie? Ply you with whisky instead? Is that what Nigel would do? Would *that* be a more manly remedy in your eyes?'

'No!' Frankie shuddered. Strong drink had been her father's escape route, the answer to every difficulty. 'No,' she repeated, 'all I want is for you to leave me alone. Stop interfering in my life. I've got enough problems,' she added savagely, 'without *you* adding to them.'

'Oh?' He was strangely still. 'In what way have *I* added to your problems?'

She could have enumerated many ways for him, principally the confusion she felt whenever he was near. Confusion which had led to vagrant, shameful thoughts and sensations she had no business to experience—at least not with Mike.

Until a few days ago, Frankie had believed she had her life neatly mapped out—career, Nigel, marriage, a safe untroubled path to a financially and emotionally secure future such as her mother had never known. And with only Mrs Greaves as a small niggling blemish on the rosy picture.

But of late she had found little doubts creeping in to

destroy this projected image—and the author of these doubts was Mike Leeming.

'How am *I* a problem to you?' Mike asked again. Once more there was only a hand's breadth between them and he was regarding her very oddly.

Frankie snapped out of her introspective mood to give him the alternative, the safe answer. 'I'm surprised you even need to ask. Donkeys, cows—and now *geese*. Mike, I will *not* have those sly, evil creatures here.'

'Oh, is *that* all!' He sounded curiously disappointed. 'I shouldn't have thought it mattered that much about the geese,' he said as he moved away again, picking up the pails yet again. 'Since you're not planning to stay. Unless. . .' He stopped and swung back to look hopefully at her. 'Unless you've had a sudden change of heart about that?'

'No,' Frankie said, trying to match his stride as he made for the house. 'In fact as soon as I've taken on some help here—which I hope will be in the next day or two—I'm off, back to London. I've already been away too long.'

'Away from the bright lights, the cameras, the brittle insecurity of your artificial life,' Mike said flatly. 'Frankly, I'm disappointed in you. This last couple of days you seemed to be shaping up, showing a bit of mettle, a bit of old Francesca's grit. Obviously it was just a flash in the pan. Young women these days seem incapable of sustained effort.' He banged the milk pails down on the kitchen floor.

'Hark at Methuselah,' Frankie taunted. 'Anyway, you've no *right* to be disappointed in me. I'm nothing to you. It's downright cheek. And I don't want your damned patronage either. I've coped because I *had* to and if I wanted to I could go on coping. I'm more capable than you give me credit for. But I *don't* want——'

'All right, all right!' He lifted a hand in a gesture of weary resignation. 'You needn't go on. You've convinced me—finally. If that's what you want—to throw away your aunt's last gift to you—I'll help you find someone to take over here. You can be away by next weekend. Perhaps it would be for the best all round.'

Frankie looked at him narrowly, amazed at his sudden capitulation, such an easy victory. Why would it be for the best *all round*?

'You sound as if you'll actually be quite glad to get rid of me,' she suggested, not quite sure how she felt about this sudden turn of events.

'Yes,' he said flatly, 'if you're still determined on leaving, you may as well get it over with as quickly as possible, for everyone's sake.'

'So that you won't need to waste any more of your valuable time on me,' Frankie retorted smartly and was illogically chagrined when he did not deny the allegation.

He semed to have forgotten about his suggestion of a cup of tea and she had an idea he would not welcome a reminder. A little forlornly, she watched him climb into his vehicle and drive away. That seemed to have been the regular pattern of their acquaintance, she thought sadly as she turned back into the house. Arrivals, confrontations, acrimonious partings.

Well, in another few days, Mike—and his disruptions—would be out of her life for good. It should have been a cheering thought, but for some reason it wasn't.

It was quite some time after his departure that Frankie realised he had left the offending geese behind, that she would have to run the gamut of their aggressive presence to give the donkeys their evening feed. It was that—the last straw—she tried to convince herself, that made her shed a few tears.

Nigel telephoned the following evening—from home, because Frankie could hear the ever-present television in the background.

Again Frankie's reactions were inconsistent. She should have been thrilled and excited to hear his voice but somehow she could not raise any enthusiasm. For the last twenty-four hours she had felt unutterably depressed.

'For heaven's sake,' Nigel demanded, 'what are you doing right down there in the sticks?' Of course he had not received her letter and she had left only a brief message with his employers.

Swiftly, she gave him a résumé of the last week's events.

'Good grief!' Nigel said. 'The old girl must have been gaga.'

'No, she wasn't! A bit eccentric perhaps.' Frankie was surprised to find herself defending her aunt's actions, considering how she had at first resented them—and the obligations they imposed upon her.

'But what on earth possessed her to leave this damned sanctuary to you? What possible use——?'

'I suppose she wasn't thinking of its usefulness. I suppose she just wanted someone she believed she could trust to——'

'You mean, she seriously expected *you* to——?'

'Don't forget,' Frankie excused her aunt, 'she hadn't seen me since I was a child. In those days——'

'You'll sell, of course.'

'No.' Frankie had been leaving this unpalatable piece of news until last.

'What? Why ever not? Lord knows why, but to some people the Cotswolds is a very desirable area. Some property developer would——'

'The land's not to be sold *or* the house. I'm supposed to live here and——'

'*Live* there!' Nigel's voice rose an outraged octave. 'Bloody ridiculous. *And* impossible. There's no way we could——'

'I didn't say I was going to,' Frankie interrupted. 'But those are the terms and if I don't fulfil them I don't get a penny.'

There was such a long silence that Frankie thought at first they had been disconnected. Then Nigel said, 'I'm coming down there. Blast! I can't make it for a day or two yet.' Obviously in the silence he had been thumbing through his diary. 'In the meantime, Frankie, don't make any rash decisions. Sit tight. I think that trustee fellow's been conning you—for his own benefit. He's probably an out and out rogue.'

'He is *not*!' Frankie said, surprised again by her own indignation, this time on Mike's behalf.

'Better leave that for *me* to decide,' Nigel said. 'Women *are* a bit gullible.'

'But Nigel——'

'Sorry, love, can't talk any longer now. Mother's

waiting to watch her programme. See you in a day or two. And hang on to what's rightfully yours.'

Frankie could understand Nigel's reaction to her news and the terms of her inheritance. She had felt exactly the same way herself—at first—about the sanctuary and about Mike. Carefully she examined that thought. Did it mean her feelings had undergone a change? And did she mean the sanctuary, or Mike, or both?

Until she had spoken to Nigel she *had* been planning an early return to London. But it wasn't just his advice that had changed her mind.

His outspoken criticism of her late aunt and his vehement denigration of the Cotswolds had put Frankie somewhat on the defensive. Not only were her loyalties now strangely divided, but, though it was all right for *her* to decide she would not live at Lionswick Farm, she felt oddly resentful at Nigel's adamant veto. And then his attitude was such a strong contrast to Mike's ardent championship of old Francesca and his enthusiasm for her scheme.

But there she went again, comparing Nigel with Mike, which was as impossible as comparing chalk to cheese.

CHAPTER SIX

FRANKIE was giving the donkeys their early morning feed when she was suddenly uncomfortably conscious of being watched. At first she thought it was Mike who had come upon her undetected and she turned sharply. But it wasn't Mike. A totally unexpected wave of disappointment swept through her.

'Can I help you?' she asked.

The two youths approached her, one with jaunty confidence, the other trailing in his wake.

'Saw your postcard in the window.' The jaunty one seemed to have elected himself spokesman. Small and wiry, he had a thin sharp face and bright intelligent eyes. The second youth, taller and heavily built, had a dull, almost vacant expression.

'You're interested in working with donkeys?' Frankie asked a little doubtfully. Somehow neither of them was quite what she had in mind.

'S'pose so,' the sharp-faced one said. 'A job's a job, ain't it? But Tony,' he pointed to his companion, 'he's barmy about animals. *I* could get *any* job,' he boasted, 'but not many folk'll have old Tone.'

'Oh? Why's that?'

''Cos they think he's not all there.' There was a note of indignation now. 'But he's all right is old Tone. He's slow but he's a worker and he'll do whatever I tell him. So, how about it, miss?'

'Well,' Frankie said slowly, 'I don't know. I mean you're the first to apply. There might be others. To be fair——'

'There won't be any others!' the sharp-faced one said with conviction. 'We talked it over, me and my mates, and we agreed, this'd suit Tone down to the ground.'

'You mean they all agreed not to apply?'

'S'right.' A cheeky grin.

Frankie was a little dismayed by this evidence of some kind of local mafia and yet there was something about the lad, the sheer nerve of him, that appealed to her sense of humour. 'And you and Tony always work together?'

'He's me brother. He needs looking after. *I* look after him,' was the simple reply.

'And what's your name?' Frankie asked.

'Sid Green.'

'Well, Sid, since you seem to have cornered the market. . .' and as he looked at her uncomprehendingly, 'since you've put everyone else off coming here, I don't seem to have much choice. So how would it be if I take you on a week's trial?'

'Suits me.' Sid shrugged. 'But I'm telling you, you won't want to get rid of us. Tone's a good worker.'

'And you?' Frankie asked.

He met her gaze steadily. 'You won't have any complaints, miss. I pull me weight.'

Frankie studied his face. Sid Green was a smooth operator. He might also be a con merchant. But on the other hand she liked his dogged loyalty to his brother. Not every lad would take his responsibilities so seriously. His was a sharp, intelligent face, but she also thought it was an honest one. She made up her mind. 'Right, Sid, suppose you and Tony start now, show me what you can do. The stables need mucking out. You'll find all the tools you need in that lean-to.'

Sid wasn't the type to grovel, Frankie thought, but she believed she detected an expression of gratitude in the keen eyes.

Promising to return later to assess their progress, she returned to the house, her arrival coinciding with that of Mike Leeming. At the sight of him she felt her heart skip a beat or two and quickly suppressed her instinctive pleasure at seeing him.

'I didn't send for you,' she said coolly as he slid from the Land Rover and strode towards her, as intimidatingly large and masculine as ever. 'All the animals are perfectly healthy.'

'I realise that.' His tone was as chilly as her own. 'I stopped by merely to give you a warning.'

'Oh?' Frankie bristled. What was he about to threaten her with this time?

'Yes. I've been making enquiries in the village among the local lads, trying to find you some help—so you can get back to the bright lights!'

He certainly hadn't wasted much time, Frankie thought bitterly. He *was* in a hurry all of a sudden to get rid of her.

'You needn't bother——' she began but he was still speaking.

'I discovered something rather disturbing. I warned you that there were some undesirable elements in the village. And one of those undesirables is a lad called Sid Green. Since he and his family moved here six months ago from London, Sid's constituted himself as some kind of gang leader. Because he's a smart operator, all the local lads defer to him. I discovered that Sid Green's earmarked this job for himself and his older brother—a thick-witted youth who does whatever Sid tells him. If they show up don't touch them with a barge-pole. They——'

'Too late,' Frankie said. She was a little dismayed at Mike's news, but delighted to be able to confound him. 'I've already hired them. They've started work.'

It was the first time she'd seen Mike momentarily at a loss for words. But it did not take him long to recover.

'Then you'd better *un*hire them.' It sounded like an order. 'You can make some excuse. Tell them——'

'I shan't do anything of the sort,' Frankie retorted. 'I don't go back on promises. I said I'd give them a trial and I will.'

'Frankie,' Mike's voice rose in exasperation, 'Sid Green may be only sixteen. But he's a crook in embryo. There's already suspicion in the village about thefts of——'

'Anything proven?'

'No, but——'

'When you've *got* proof,' Frankie said, 'come and see me again. Until then, Sid and Tony stay.'

His rugged face hardened. 'You seriously intend to leave those two, unsupervised, while you——'

'They won't be unsupervised. *I'll* be here to keep an eye on them.'

There was another silence, a longer one this time.

Then, 'I thought you were leaving Lionswick. I thought you couldn't wait to get back to——'

'I can't,' Frankie agreed. She did not want to tell him about Nigel's impending visit.

Despite her own earlier doubts, she now believed that Mike had dealt honestly with her over her aunt's will. But it would do no harm to let Nigel make his own assessment. That was his right as her fiancé.

'I can't wait,' she said again, 'but since my agent doesn't have any work for me at present. . .' Then, seeing the sudden gleam in Mike's eye, 'And don't you dare say you told me so. It's only a temporary thing. I shall be as busy as ever in a week or two.' Behind her back, superstitiously, she crossed her fingers. 'But in the meantime I can stay here and get Sid and Tony settled in. I liked them and as far as I'm concerned they're innocent until proved guilty.'

Mike stared at her for a long time and Frankie held his steely grey gaze, determined not to flinch. To her surprise he gave a sudden bark of laughter.

'Well, so there *is* something of your aunt in you after all. She would have stood up for those lads just as you have. The only trouble is I'd back her judgement of character against yours.'

'Really?' Frankie said in a deceptively mild tone of voice. Then, 'But I was spot-on when I assessed *your* character.'

His eyes narrowed. 'And what does *that* mean exactly?' There was a note in his voice that made Frankie quiver suddenly, and while she was not going to back down she decided not to pursue the point.

'Oh,' airily, 'I don't think I need to go into detail.'

'Don't you?' he said grimly. 'Well, *I* think you do. You can't make remarks like that, my girl, and then not be prepared to substantiate them. I held back on you the other day, but maybe now would be as good an opportunity as any for us to have a frank exchange of opinions.' He gestured peremptorily towards the house. 'Shall we?'

The whole thing sounded frighteningly ominous and Frankie was sharp-tongued to cover an attack of nerves. 'It's up to *me* to invite *you*. Not the other way round. After all, this is *my* house.'

'Not for much longer. Not if you're leaving,' he reminded her, and before she could voice any further protest he had unceremoniously preceded her through the back door.

Frankie was determined not to offer him hospitality this time and she sat down before he could suggest that she make coffee. But this did not deter him one whit. Instead, he set about preparing it himself, and it was not until two steaming mugs were standing on the table before them that he spoke again.

'Well?'

'Well, what?' she fenced.

'Your assessment of my character. Let's hear it.' He sat across from her, watching her intently.

A few days ago Frankie would have given him her opinion frankly and fearlessly and it would have been a distinctly unflattering one. But though her opinion had modified itself she wasn't about to admit it and, besides, she was oddly afraid of provoking him. Mike could be very unpredictable.

He might just laugh at her as he had done once or

twice. Or. . . Or he might take it into his head to
retaliate, to punish her for her outspokenness. And at
the thought of the form his punishments had taken in
the past, Frankie quivered.

'You. . .you wouldn't like it,' she told him.

'Nevertheless.'

She tried diversionary tactics. 'You mentioned a
"frank exchange". *You* can go first if you like.'

Mike looked at her quizzically. 'You seem suddenly
unsure of your ground. Why could that be, I wonder?'
And as she did not answer, 'All right, if that's the way
you want it, I'll tell you what *I* think of *you*.'

But he was a long time in fulfilling this promise. As
he rose and began to prowl about the kitchen, Frankie
watched him, her nervous anticipation growing by the
moment. Whatever he was going to say she doubted
that it would be complimentary.

But did she *want* compliments? On the rare occasions
when Mike had evidenced admiration, either by look
or word, she had felt distinctly uneasy.

When he did begin to speak he was out of sight,
behind her. And yet Frankie's senses told her that he
was only an inch or two away. She dared not look
round at him but continued to stare straight ahead, her
hands tightly clasping the coffee-mug.

'It surprises me how difficult I find it to give a
detached analysis of your character,' Mike said. 'Nat-
urally I'd formed an idea before we even met. I knew
you'd be beautiful, of course. Your aunt's clippings had
shown me that.'

He had moved to stand right behind her chair now

and his hands came to rest on her shoulders. They were heavy, warm, restraining.

Frankie sat very still, scarcely breathing.

'The photographs didn't do you justice,' Mike went on, his fingers absently kneading as he spoke, his voice strangely husky. 'You're far lovelier in the flesh. But. . .'

In the prolonged silence, Frankie somehow found her voice.

'But?' she croaked.

'But in other ways you're very different from what I expected.'

Frankie digested that for a few moments. She was well aware that, before they'd met, Mike had prejudged her. She knew that he had been prejudiced against her because of what he had seen as her neglect of her aunt. Yet she honestly believed that she had convinced him it was not deliberate but due to circumstances.

It didn't take much intelligence to realise that he had pictured her as being selfish and uncaring. But what else had he expected?

'I expected to thoroughly dislike you.'

Frankie jumped. It was uncanny, just as if he had read her mind.

'I thought you'd be hard, sophisticated, vain and spoiled beyond redemption.' One finger was caressing the nape of her downbent neck and Frankie closed her eyes, hypnotised by his touch, wanting it to go on and on.

'But you've decided,' she said shakily, 'that there's hope for me yet?'

'You have a veneer,' Mike continued almost as if she had not spoken. 'But it *is* only a veneer. Underneath it you're as soft as marshmallow. Aren't you?' he demanded suddenly.

The finger had stopped its insidious mesmerism. His hands were at her shoulders once more but this time with a biting grip, pulling her up, turning her, so that she was forced to look at him.

'Aren't you?' he repeated, and as she did not answer he gave her a little shake. 'Frankie, answer me. Why do you pretend to be something you're not?'

'I. . . I don't.' Frankie was genuinely surprised. 'At least I don't think so.'

'You do,' he contradicted. 'If you were the hard-boiled young woman I was expecting, one look at this place would have been enough. You would have turned right round and gone back to London, regardless of the hardship to the donkeys, regardless of anything I said. But you didn't go. You stayed. *And* you coped. That says a lot in my book.'

'It doesn't mean——'

But he swept on inexorably. 'And however much you try to hide it, you *do* have a caring nature. Like your aunt. If that donkey had died the other night, you'd have broken your heart. You cared enough too for old Jed's feelings, enough not to argue with me in front of him.'

Frankie was speechless again. This rapid, almost tempestuous accolade was not at all what she had expected. It sounded as if. . .as if Mike had actually grown to *like* her.

That was fine by her, she decided. Frankie liked to

be liked and his former attitude had hurt. Principally, she told herself, because he'd believed things of her that were not true. But—and she had to be honest with herself at least—it had also hurt because Mike was so eminently likeable himself, someone about whose opinion she had come to care.

Oh, not at first. At first she had detested him as heartily as he had her. But her attitude had changed, perhaps more swiftly than his. She was. . . Yes, she was quite. . .quite fond of Mike.

And what a feeble word *that* was, she scoffed at herself. It scarcely described her reactions where he was concerned. But then Mike was only a friend. It was important to remember that.

'And now,' Mike said, again making her start, for the taut silence between them had stretched on for so long, deepening in intensity, while they held each other's gaze. 'Now,' he said, 'it's your turn. . .'

Frankie stared at him blankly. Her turn to what? She had quite forgotten the original starting-point of this particular confrontation.

'. . .to tell me what *you* think of *me*,' Mike concluded.

'I. . . I. . .' Frankie's voice felt strangely constricted in her throat and she cleared it nervously, moistening her lips with the tip of her tongue. She had to say something. She knew Mike would not let her get away with it. 'You're. . .you're a bit of a mixture yourself,' she offered at last. 'Sometimes you're odiously overbearing, as though you think you know better than anyone else. Sometimes you're kind—very kind. Sometimes you make me furiously angry. Sometimes you make me laugh.'

'And you still haven't decided whether you like me or not,' Mike said. He sounded put out. 'And yet a little while ago you were priding yourself on your judgement of character. So do you or don't you?'

Frankie wondered what was wrong with her. It was not normal for her to so easily lose the thread of a conversation.

'Do I or don't I what?' she murmured hazily.

'Like me, dammit!' He said it with sudden impatience.

It was quite impossible now to unlink her gaze from his, and prickles of perspiration broke out on her skin. She cleared her throat, trying to ease its dry tension, smoothed suddenly damp palms against her jeans.

'I. . . I don't know,' she said, aware that it was a feeble effort. And untruthful at that. Because she did know.

'Maybe,' his voice was menacingly soft now, 'maybe you need some help deciding?'

As his head came closer and closer, his eyes searching her face, observing her reactions, Frankie felt as though her breath was suspended somewhere in her throat. As she stared at his mouth, the full but shapely bottom lip, her heart was pumping at ten times its normal rate, her pulses keeping pace. Mike was so potently male. She knew what he was about and she knew she ought to scream out to him to stop. But the only sound she could produce was a small, inarticulate, pleading cry, her fists clenched against his chest.

Slowly his hands moved down from her shoulders to curl about and almost span her waist, holding her against him, so that she could feel the heat of his strong body even through her jeans and the thick sweater. Then his mouth was hard and determined on hers.

This was no tentative kiss. It was not even like the previous occasions when he had kissed her. Then he had been either angry or teasing. He was neither now.

For a moment she resisted the hypnotic rising tide of sensuality. But as one of his hands moved to shape and caress her breast she was engulfed in a wave of sensation, melting against him so completely that physical awareness blanked off all that her brain was trying to tell her. Her tense fingers uncurled and glided up over his chest, pausing where his heartbeat thudded rhythmically beneath her palms.

At her submission Mike gave a small growl of satisfaction deep in his throat and thirstily his tongue probed her parted lips. Hitherto, Frankie had always disliked a kiss that employed a thrusting tongue. With Nigel, because he was her fiancé, she had endured it. But with Mike it was different. No endurance was necessary and after a moment her own tongue responded, licking, caressing, duelling with his.

She had never been kissed quite like this, never experienced such sensations. Even Nigel had never affected her in this way. The realisation of what a kiss could be like totally overwhelmed her senses. Small sounds of pleasure rose from deep inside her and her hands continued the upward movement they had begun, sliding into the thick wavy hair at his nape while she allowed him to go on tasting and plundering her mouth.

After what seemed an eternity of feeling and when Frankie could think of nothing she wanted more than to be a part of him, he raised his head for a moment. 'I want you, Frankie. Dammit, I want you.' And there was a surprised note in his voice as he said, 'But I believe *you* want me?'

Oh, yes, she wanted him. Frankie had finally to admit, if only to herself, that this was what all her earlier confusion had been about. Even when she had disliked and mistrusted Mike, her body had responded to his allure. She had known before he spoke that she was not alone in her desire. His kiss had become an expression of a powerful physical need. She had felt his arousal, hard, explicit and demanding against her. But the way she felt was wrong, what she was doing was wrong.

Mike posed a danger to the future she had planned for herself, every instinct bar one was telling her that. But still that one instinct clamoured for the satisfaction she knew he could give her.

'You want me, Frankie, don't you?' Mike insisted huskily.

What she would have replied Frankie had no idea for at that moment the back door opened, letting in a gust of cold wintry air.

'We've finished mucking out, miss,' Sid's cheerful cockney voice told her. 'What d'you want us to do next?'

With a stifled oath Mike released her and swung round to look at the two lads, Sid already over the threshold, his brother hovering outside.

'I didn't hear you knock,' Mike grated. He was making a valiant effort to hide his aroused condition but Frankie guessed the astute Sid wasn't missing much.

Her fears were confirmed. 'Didn't know she'd be snogging at this time of day, did I?' he responded.

Frankie was torn between laughter and frustration. Her lower body still ached for the incitement so recently proffered by Mike's, but her head was rapidly clearing now that she was free of his potent aura and she supposed she ought to be grateful to Sid. He had saved her from committing the worst crime in her book—disloyalty.

If Sid had not interrupted when he did, she might—in the heat of the moment of course—have said and done something for which she would never forgive herself.

She moved towards the old-fashioned stove. 'If you've mucked out all those stalls so quickly,' she said, 'I think you've earned yourself some elevenses. Coffee, tea, hot chocolate?' she asked, her hand poised over the canisters.

'Ain't you got nothin' stronger?' Sid enquired. 'A beer would be favourite.'

'I'm afraid not. And even if I had I wouldn't encourage you to drink alcohol at your age.'

Sid shrugged. 'Coffee it is, then. But I been drinkin' beer since I was twelve and so's he.' He indicated his brother. 'Come on in, Tone,' he urged as he sat down at the kitchen table, totally at ease with himself and his surroundings.

Frankie dared not look at Mike to see how he was reacting to this incursion on what until now had been his undisputed territory.

'Will you have another drink, Mike, before you go?' she asked over her shoulder.

'No, thanks.' He was curt. 'I'm late as it is. But before I do go I want a word with you, my lad.' He stood over Sid, so much larger, his manner so ominous that Frankie felt quite sorry for the boy.

But Sid Green was not easy to intimidate.

'Oh, yeah?' he enquired, his mouth already full of the biscuits Frankie had placed before him.

'Yes. I understand that Miss Latimer has agreed to give you a trial—you and your brother. Now Miss Latimer is a friend of mine——'

'So I noticed, guv!' Sid winked at Frankie and she choked back a giggle. Mike was in no mood for frivolity. And she couldn't blame him. If he'd felt only half the way she had it must be no easy matter for him to speak and act normally.

'Miss Latimer is a friend of mine,' Mike repeated grimly. 'And I shall be keeping a close eye on things here—and on *you*. If I find that you've repaid her kindness with ingratitude, I'll have your hide. Just remember that.' And to Frankie he said, 'I'll see you later. We have some unfinished business.' And, slamming the door behind him, he was gone.

'Sorry about that, miss,' Sid said, 'interruptin' yer love-life, I mean.

'It's all right, Sid. But perhaps, another time, it *would* be a good idea to knock.'

He nodded briefly, then, 'Why d'yer keep donkeys, miss?'

'Because they were left to me, by my aunt.'

'Yeah, I know that. But what d'yer do with 'em now you've got 'em?'

'Do with them?' Frankie looked vaguely at him. Her mind was still half on Mike, still torn between guilt and. . .yes. . .disappointment that his lovemaking had not reached its natural conclusion.

'Well, d'yer give donkey rides—at garden feets, like? When Tone was at his special school near 'ere,' Sid went on, 'they used ter take kids ter the seaside and give 'em donkey rides. They 'ave 'orse riding fer the 'andicapped too in some places, don't they?'

'Yes.' He had all of Frankie's attention now. 'You know that's rather a good idea of yours, Sid. I mean there's nothing wrong with these donkeys. They're in good condition. But all they do is eat their heads off all day.'

'Tone's too big fer ridin' 'em now,' Sid went on, 'but there's a lot of little kids at that school. And they could bring 'em in, in buses, couldn't they?'

Frankie sat down, elbows resting on the table, her chin propped in her hands as she looked thoughtfully at him. If she had been planning to stay at the sanctuary, Sid's was just the kind of idea that would have appealed to her.

Old Francesca's donkeys had been rescued from hardship and deprivation. They lived the life of Riley at Lionswick. Why shouldn't they repay their debt to society by providing a service to those who suffered another kind of deprivation?

'We could 'elp, miss.' It was the first time Tony had spoken. Frankie hadn't even been sure that he *could* speak. Now he was looking at her with real animation in his hitherto rather blank face. 'We could 'old the little 'uns on, so they didn't fall.'

'The problem is, Sid and Tony,' Frankie said, 'that I'm not staying on here. I have a job in town. And my fiancé doesn't like the country. So——'

'What? Him who was here just now? The vet? Doesn't like the country?' Sid sounded incredulous.

Frankie felt herself blushing as she explained that Mike Leeming was not her fiancé. And Sid's expressive, 'Oh, yeah?' said everything.

'So you see,' she went on hastily, 'I'm not sure your idea would work. I mean, whoever takes over here might not like the idea or be prepared to spend the time on it.' She looked at their crestfallen faces. 'Look,' she promised, 'I'll talk to Mr Leeming about it next time he's here. If *he* thinks it's a good idea, perhaps. . . Well, anyway, I'll let you know, I promise. And now let's go and see what sort of a job you've made of those stables.'

Frankie could find no fault with the boys' efforts. In fact she had to admit that they had mucked out far more efficiently than she had ever done herself. There was plenty of maintenance needed around the property and having set them to work once more she returned to the house.

It was only then that she realised that having two extra pairs of hands to help had left her at something of a loose end.

Living in a small, easily maintained flat, she had been totally unprepared for the amount of housework a larger house would involve. And with the animals taking up most of her daylight hours, chores—when she had any energy left—had been done at night. Now, she realised, she had several hours at her disposal.

She made herself another coffee and sat down in her freshly painted and gleaming kitchen. It was surprising what a difference a coat of paint and her efforts at cleaning had made to the room's atmosphere. Now it was quite a cheerful place to be.

A few days ago she would have welcomed a period of idleness. But not now. Inactivity left too much time for thinking—thinking in particular about Mike Leeming and his recent startling behaviour.

He had promised he would be back. And to Frankie that promise seemed more like a threat—a threat to the discipline she *must* impose more firmly upon herself.

She had always been scornful of girls who—having left boyfriends behind them at home—had indulged in holiday romances. In her opinion it showed a total lack of integrity and Frankie had never for one moment imagined that she could be capable of such behaviour. Moreover she did not have the excuse of a heady romantic setting to tempt her from the paths of loyalty. Nothing could be *less* romantic than the position in which she now found herself.

And yet, if, when Mike walked into the farmhouse again, he was to recommence his sensual assault upon her, she feared her resolution would crumble as easily as it had done before.

If it were not for the fact of Nigel's promised visit, she ought to leave here immediately. A telephone call from her agent had held out the promise of a modelling job—if she was prepared to dye her hair blonde. It was not an idea Frankie relished. She was rather proud of her Titian tresses. Yet perhaps she ought to put financial considerations before vanity?

But she could not sit here indefinitely, brooding on possibilities and, even more dangerously, waiting for Mike to erupt into her life once more. Purposefully, she set down her empty cup and stood up. There was still some paint left. She would begin on the dark dingy hallway that connected kitchen to living area.

It really was gratifying, she thought an hour or so later, just how much improvement her efforts were making. Unfortunately she did not have enough paint to finish the job, which would mean another trip to town. She found herself singing a cheerful little song as she slapped on the last few brushfuls.

For a short while she really *had* managed to put the problem of Mike to the back of her mind, so that she was startled, feeling her heart thud erratically, her stomach performing similar gymnastics, when she heard his voice calling from the back door.

CHAPTER SEVEN

'FRANKIE! Frankie? Oh, there you are.' At the sight of her, perched precariously on the top of the stepladder, Mike stopped short, filling the doorway with his broad frame.

This time it did not bother Frankie that he should catch her looking her worst. By now she knew that, unlike Nigel, such things did not matter to Mike. If Mike liked someone it was for themselves, not for their hairstyle or apparel.

'You're extending your operations, then?' Mike sounded inordinately pleased.

'Only to finish up the paint,' she said quickly. 'I hate waste.'

'So do I,' he said, but with a peculiar emphasis she did not understand. He did not leave her long in doubt. 'And *you're* wasting yourself, Frankie, if you go back to London and that mindless job of yours. You have it in you to really make something of this old place—a home as well as a sanctuary.'

As she made to descend the ladder, he held out a helping hand. There was no need for her to accept it. The ladder was perfectly steady. But it would be unnecessarily churlish to ignore that extended hand. Taking a deep, calming breath, Frankie put her fingers into his.

As she reached ground-level, she expected him to

release her and move away. But he did not and Frankie found herself trapped between the stepladder and his formidably large figure; and immediately her senses were ensnared by the warm masculine emanations proceeding from him, his musky erotic scent.

'Ex-excuse me,' she stammered, trying to side-step him. 'I. . . I have to put this brush in to soak.'

He stepped aside, but his throaty chuckle told her he was not deceived. He followed her into the kitchen, hard on her heels.

'Sid and Tony have worked really hard today,' Frankie rattled on, determined not to let any conversation begin, other than that of the most trivial nature.

She moved to the sink, and concentrated hard on eliminating every trace of paint from the brush.

He followed her, stood close behind her, bending over her as if to see that she was performing her task thoroughly, but only succeeding in making her aware of him with every fibre of her being.

'Where *are* those two lads?' he asked, his finger toying with a tendril of hair that curled provocatively at the nape of her downbent neck.

'M-mending paddock fences.' Waves of heat swept through her and her hands shook as she rinsed and dried the paintbrush.

'They're well out of the way, then,' he said with satisfaction. 'Good! We don't want any more unscheduled interruptions.'

Frankie wished desperately that Sid and Tony would appear. 'I. . . I think their working here is going to be a success,' she told Mike huskily and now she busied herself in cleaning the paint splashes from the sink.

'Maybe,' he said non-committally. He was threading a hand through her hair now, in a sensuous stroking movement as though he was deriving as much pleasure from the exercise as she, unwillingly, had to admit she felt.

'I. . . I like them,' she went on a little desperately. 'And. . .and Sidney had a very good idea. He. . .he thinks I should use the donkeys to give rides to the disabled and mentally handicapped. He——' She broke off as two large hands came to rest on her shoulders—large, warm and very compelling. She swallowed and forced herself to continue. 'He says there's a school near here. T-Tony went there.' Her fingers holding the cloth had stilled, her total concentration going backward to the man who stood behind her, his body just brushing hers, yet as disturbing as though its full weight rested upon her.

'Frankie!' His voice was deep, authoritative.

'I. . . I said I'd talk to you about it.'

'Frankie, look at me.'

Still she resisted. 'D-do *you* think it might be——?'

'Frankie! Shut up!' Slowly, but inexorably, he was turning her towards him.

She knew his eyes were upon her flushed face but she kept hers downcast, refusing to meet that penetrating grey gaze.

'I promised Sid——'

'Frankie,' he interrupted again, 'I didn't come back here this afternoon to talk about donkeys. I'm willing to discuss your idea, of course but——'

'S-Sid's idea.'

'*Later*,' he said fiercely. 'First we're going to talk about *us*.'

'There's nothing to talk about.' Her head was still stubbornly lowered but now a large insistent finger hooked her chin upwards and her reluctant lids fluttered up, her breath catching in her throat as she saw his expression.

'*I* think there is,' Mike said, 'I think we have a great deal to talk about. This morning——'

'Should never have happened,' Frankie said quickly. She tried, unsuccessfully, to free herself.

'That's a ridiculous thing to say.' He sounded angry. 'It did happen and now we have to consider the implications. At least *you* do. I've spent all afternoon thinking about it. And lord knows I never expected to feel that way about you. But I do. And *you* felt it too. So don't try to deny it. The thing is, what are you going to do about it?'

'*Me*? *Do*?' Frankie knew her note of indignation had made her voice shrill but she couldn't help that. 'What do you expect me to do? Why should *I* do *anything*?'

'I think you know what—and why,' Mike said gravely. 'You have an honest nature, Frankie—a trait you shared with your aunt. You wouldn't want to live a lie, now would you?' The finger that had lifted her chin was now absently tracing the contours of her face—temples, cheekbones, the dark well-defined brows, the full lower lip.

'I. . . I don't understand.' Perhaps if her brain had not been totally bemused by his proximity, by his touch, she might have been able to think more clearly, but she really did not anticipate his next words.

You wouldn't want to live a lie—with Nigel—when you feel the way you do about *me*. It's only fair you should tell him——'

'Oh! Oh, you. . .you. . .arrogant——' Words failed her.

But Frankie's gasp of outrage drew a cynical smile. 'Oh, come on, Frankie. You're not a naïve teenager. You know what this morning was all about. If we hadn't been interrupted when we were——'

'Nothing would have happened!' she snapped, jerking her head away, her nerves taut bowstrings as she fought back the sensations he was arousing. 'I wouldn't have let it. I'm engaged to Nigel. I'm going to marry him.' And, a little less certainly, 'I. . . I *love* him.'

'Then how,' sarcastically, 'do you rationalise the way you felt this morning?'

'I don't. I mean. . . It was a purely physical reaction.'

'Pure?' Amused, raised eyebrows mocked her.

'All right! Then it was the opposite. *Impure*! And I'm heartily ashamed of myself. But just because I. . . I. . .'

'Wanted me to make love to you?'

'No such thing,' she denied. 'You. . .you took unfair advantage. You're an experienced man and I won't deny you have a. . .a certain attraction. But there's more to love than that.'

'Such as?' he enquired. He was holding her by the shoulders again now and a strangely weak Frankie seemed to have no strength to thrust him away.

'L-liking, respect, shared interests and aims.'

'How very clinical,' he sneered. 'Poor Nigel—if *that's* all he gets from you.'

'Of course that's not all,' she snapped unwarily. 'I——'

'You've made love—in every sense of the word?' Mike's grip tightened, as did the lines of his mouth and jaw. He jerked her towards him, her body arched so that though they touched at every point from chest to thigh, her head and shoulders were thrust backwards, so that he could glare fiercely into her eyes.

'Whether I have or not, it's none of your business,' somehow Frankie found the breath to say.

'Oh, no?' he asked softly, menacingly.

'*No!*'

'But you see, Frankie, I don't agree with you. I think it *is* my business. It became very much my business this morning, when I realised there was no way I'm going to let you go out of my life—Nigel or no Nigel.'

His insistence was beginning to anger her and anger lent her the strength to fight the insidious weakness his closeness had produced.

'Please let go of me,' she said coldly, 'and stop talking such utter nonsense. I've already told you, this morning should never have happened. And nothing like that is going to happen ever again.'

His wolfish grin was the only warning she had of what was about to happen.

His breath was hot and sweet in the instant before his mouth burned against hers, his teeth biting, tugging on her lips, his tongue an invasive force, exploring the inner sensitive lining.

Frankie struggled, beating her clenched hands against his broad chest, trying desperately to kick his shins. But for all the impression she made he might have been hewn of stone. His only response was to deepen the kiss, to haul her trembling body even closer against the hard insistence of his.

Excitement licked her body with a slow consuming flame. 'Mike, please, don't,' she whispered brokenly. But her plea went unheeded.

For a moment longer she resisted, but she was only flesh and blood, her body seeming to possess a will of its own, and from almost their first meeting this man had been demonstrating his effect upon her. Then, reason and sanity deserting her, helplessly she was returning his kisses, shivering as she felt his immediate response to her submission, his excitement igniting her own.

And now his urgency was echoed by hers, her fingers deeply plunged into his hair as she arched against him, inviting him to plunder still further. She was lost, drowning in passion, feeling perspiration break out all over her body as his hands slid over her, grasping her hips, forcing her to feel the hardness of his arousal.

His hands became even more demanding, pushing up beneath her sweater, caressing satiny flesh, becoming impatient with the barrier of her bra, groaning as he discovered the hardened nipples, tormenting them until Frankie thought she must faint from sheer desire.

'*Have* you slept with Nigel, Frankie?' Mike demanded huskily. 'Have you?' He shook her a little, increasing her dizziness.

'No,' Frankie whispered, the answer produced by some force she was powerless to resist. 'No, I haven't.'

She heard him growl his satisfaction and knew she was lost. But, to her infinite surprise, he released her, setting her down on a chair as the world still spun crazily round her.

She looked up at him wonderingly, the pit of her stomach aching with frustration.

'Now I know that for certain, I'm content to wait,' Mike told her, his chest still rising and falling as slowly he regained his own self-control.

'To. . .to wait?' Frankie stammered uncomprehendingly.

'Until you've given Nigel his marching orders, dammit.'

Frankie parted her lips to protest, then found she couldn't. Right at that moment she could not honestly say what course of action she would follow. Surely her loyalty was still to Nigel. And yet was it any use denying what her heart told her? That her feelings for Nigel Greaves now seemed a very pallid thing beside the way she felt for Mike.

She tried again. 'Mike, I——' But at that moment the back door opened.

'Oh, crumbs!' Sid Green's dismayed voice was heard to say. '*He's* here again. Sorry, miss.' He began to back out but his larger brother blocked his progress, giving Frankie time to seize upon this reprieve.

'Sid, Tony, it's all right. Come in. I. . . I've told Mr Leeming about your idea, Sid. But perhaps you'd like to talk to him about it yourself? Mike,' she dared not look directly at him, 'would you be an angel and give these two a lift home? They must be tired out and it's getting dark. I'm sure their mother would be grateful.'

He gave her a sardonic look which told her he was

not deceived for a moment. But he complied with her request.

As the door closed behind Mike and the Green brothers, Frankie sank into a chair with a silent whistle of relief. She knew that once again she had come perilously close to abandoning all she believed in.

This. . .this *chemistry* between herself and Mike—for that was all it was—had nearly led her into making an appalling mistake.

How long had she known Mike Leeming? Less than two weeks. How long had she known Nigel? Nearly two years. And yet for one mad, reckless moment she had actually been considering giving Nigel his *congé*—just on the strength of a few kisses and a demand from Mike—a demand he had no right to make.

What did she know about Mike? She knew his occupation, knew he had a fiery temper when roused, a temper to match her own. *She* needed a man with a calm, equable temperament, to balance her own volatility. She didn't want a marriage rent by dissension. She and Nigel might argue occasionally but there was never any *passion* in their disagreements.

She shuddered suddenly. That was something else she knew about Mike. He was capable of passion, but this time she was thinking of the sexual kind. Making love with Mike would certainly never be dull.

The thought brought her up short. Did that mean she found Nigel's lovemaking dull? No. No, of course not. It was just that Nigel was. . .well, restrained. He respected her. He was always the gentleman. Nigel had never handled her so fiercely, nor kissed her so intensely. Once or twice he had initiated more intimate caresses. But at a sign of displeasure from her, her stipulation that those touches should be saved until after they were married, he had always desisted.

And yet. . .and yet she had allowed Mike to touch her and she had enjoyed that touch, had even craved a prolongation, further intimacies. Thinking about it, she could recall exactly how she had felt and incredulously she knew that just the thought had made her nipples tinglingly hard once more.

She sank her head in her hands. Oh, lord, what was happening to her?

It must be the loneliness. She wasn't used to such isolation. She was missing Nigel, in a situation where there were unfamiliar responsibilities and anxieties. She had come to rely on Mike, that was all. Their earlier hostility towards each other had been resolved and propinquity had done the rest.

She was no better than those girls she despised, with their holiday romances. Just because Nigel was out of sight it didn't mean he should be out of mind. Determinedly she stood up and made for the telephone. She would call Nigel. The sound of his voice would restore everything to normal.

Two minutes later she put the telephone down once more. She should have known. Mrs Greaves had answered. Nigel wasn't home yet. And when he did come in, his mother had said with palpable satisfaction, he wouldn't have time to make phone calls. He would be going straight out again—to the theatre.

As Frankie sat down again, she upbraided herself for her suspicious mind. Just because Nigel was going to the theatre was no reason to suspect him of infidelity.

But Nigel hated live theatre, the little voice of suspicion reminded her. He much preferred a film. Even more so when he could watch it on television in his own home. He really *did* have a lot in common with his mother.

Perhaps the theatre visit was in the line of business? He did sometimes entertain clients.

Oh, bother it! It was no use sitting here brooding. If she wasn't having unsuitable thoughts about Mike she was having disloyal ones about Nigel. The best remedy lay in work. She might as well start cleaning up the living-room. Her improvements had not reached that far as yet.

She swept, dusted and polished until she was physically exhausted. But manual tasks did not occupy the brain and she took her restless thoughts to bed with her.

It was the thumping on the back door, plus a hail of pebbles raining against her window, that alerted Frankie to the realisation that she had overslept. It must have been three in the morning before she had finally dropped off.

An anguished glance at her wristwatch on the bedside table told her that it was eight-thirty. It was a wonder the donkeys hadn't woken her. Usually they were braying for their morning feed long before this.

The very fact of their silence was alarming. With visions of Mike's reactions if some disaster had occurred, she threw open the bedroom window, letting in a bitterly cold blast of air. It was almost cold enough for snow.

'You all right, miss?' It was Sid's anxious face gazing up at her, and relief mingled with disappointment.

'Yes. Yes, thanks. Just overdone it, I'm afraid. I'll be down in a minute.'

She dressed in double-quick time, then ran down to the kitchen to let the boys in.

'The donkeys must be starving,' she said anxiously.

'They'll be OK, miss.' Sid was cheerful. 'When we saw you wasn't about, we turned 'em out into the paddocks. Thought a bit of grass was better than leavin' 'em to starve. Tone and me'll lug the bran out to 'em there when it's ready.'

'We thought somethin' 'ad 'appened to you, miss,' Tony put in. 'Thought you was sick or somethin'.'

Frankie felt warmed by the boys' concern.

'Have you had *your* breakfast?' she asked as she put the kettle on. 'But I suppose you must have?'

'We 'ave. But we could go another, miss,' Sid said eagerly. 'There's six of us kids, so the 'elpin's aren't so big.'

'Goodness,' Frankie said as she hunted out extra plates and took half a dozen eggs from the antiquated fridge. 'How on earth do you all fit into that tiny cottage?'

'Mum and Dad 'ave the front bedroom and our Sonia—she's only two—she sleeps with 'em. Gran's in the back bedroom with our Lucy. Sam, Willie, me and Tone 'ave the box-room. It's a bit of a squash.'

'It must be,' Frankie agreed sympathetically.

'When me and Tone 'ave saved up enough, we're goin' to get a place of our own.'

Frankie admired Sid's spirit but her heart ached for

him. She wondered if he had any idea how much the humblest abode would cost them.

She set their breakfast before them and watched with awe as her entire supply of bacon and eggs was swiftly demolished.

'Right, Tone!' Sid thrust back his chair. 'You wash up and me and Miss Latimer'll make the mash.'

'Did you talk to Mr Leeming about your idea?' Frankie asked later, as the three of them carried the bran mash out to the paddocks. 'About rides for the handicapped, I mean.'

'Yeah. He thought it were a good idea. He said he'd be up later to talk to you about it. He knows the school. He said he'd take you there.'

At this intimation Frankie's stomach gave a panicky little lurch. 'Do *you* know the way there, Sid?'

'O'course,' he said scornfully. 'Used ter visit Tony regular, didn't I?'

'Then how would it be if the three of us—you, me and Tony, drove over this morning?'

'What about *him*—the veterinary?'

'Oh, I think we can manage without him,' Frankie said airily. Even to herself she was not willing to admit that she was running scared of seeing Mike again.

So it was arranged. With the donkeys fed, all other chores were postponed until the afternoon and, well before Mike could possibly have finished morning surgery, the three of them drove out of Lionswick village. Tony sat beside Frankie in the sports car and the smaller Sid squeezed into what passed for a rear seat.

New World, the school for handicapped children,

had once been a gracious old family home in a delight-
ful setting and it was still an attractive place, despite an
obvious lack of funds for maintenance and repairs.

Frankie and her companions were received warmly
by the headmistress who remembered Tony Green.
They were given a conducted tour of the premises so
that Tony might renew some old acquaintances with
staff and pupils. Frankie's heart was touched by the
children she met, all of them handicapped in some way,
some more severely than others. And when they
returned to the head's study, she broached the subject
of their visit.

She was surprised when the elderly woman's face
fell. But the reason was soon evident.

'Oh, dear, it's a lovely idea, but I'm afraid we just
couldn't afford it.'

'There wouldn't be any charge,' Frankie said hastily.

'It's not just that, my dear. You see, we don't have
any transport now. We used to have an old minibus but
I'm afraid it just wore out. And there's no money for a
new one.'

Frankie looked at the three downcast faces and
almost before she realised what she was doing she had
committed herself to a course of action.

'That can be taken care of,' she said. 'My aunt left
me a great deal of money—certainly enough to buy a
minibus. So that's no problem.'

As she drove away from the school, Frankie realised
more fully what she had just done. She had in effect
committed herself to staying on at Lionswick. Only by
staying would she qualify for the money she had
mentioned. If she went away there was no guarantee

that a substitute caretaker would authorise the purchase of a minibus, a project which would bring in no
financial return to the sanctuary.

But with this realisation came a deeper one and with
it almost a sense of relief that her internal warring was
over. She hadn't expected to adapt so readily to country
life. But Mike was right—people did not change in the
basic essentials of their character. As a child she had
loved the country and animals. Insidiously that old love
had crept back to claim her. When she had first come
to Lionswick Farm she had resented the responsibilities
thrust upon her. But the last few days had brought
about a change in her outlook. She had actually been
enjoying her work, not only with the donkeys, but in
trying to make the old farmhouse a habitable place
once more.

How much did this change of heart have to do with
Mike? The thought leaped unbidden to her mind.
Nothing at all, she refuted hotly. It was her own
decision.

And how would Nigel react? With a confidence born
of her own enthusiasm, Frankie felt sure she could coax
Nigel into making Lionswick their home. A little gentle
blackmail perhaps? He hadn't wanted her to go on with
her modelling work after they were married. Well, she
would promise to give all that up. And he didn't *need*
to be London-based for his work. Most of it entailed
travelling around the country, something he could do
just as well from here.

And what about his mother, a niggling little voice
asked. His mother would have to lump it. Frankie had

never had any intention in any case of living in her
mother-in-law's pocket.

A mood of euphoria swept over her and she spoke
over her shoulder to Sidney. 'How about lunch out
while we're at it? To celebrate?'

By the time they set off for Lionswick again both boys
shared her growing sense of excitement. Over lunch
she had expanded upon her plans for the sanctuary.

'And I've thought of a way we can make money to
help it pay its way,' she told them. 'We'll start a
holiday-boarding service for small pets. There's nothing
like that in the area. There are a lot of outbuildings I
haven't even inspected yet. But I'm sure we could do a
conversion job on them—cages and runs and so on.
And you two,' she told them, 'are permanently hired
from now on. But I warn you, it's going to be hard
work.'

'We ain't afraid of work, miss,' Sid said stoutly.

As they bumped their way up the rutted drive to the
house a familiar vehicle came towards them. Mike's
Land Rover. He stopped, slewed across the sports car's
path and jumped down. Frankie didn't need a second
look to see that he was extremely annoyed. For her
own part, her heart was beating a frenetic rhythm.

'Where have you been? I told Sid I'd be over after
morning surgery. Didn't you pass on the message?' he
accused the boy.

'Don't blame Sid,' Frankie said quickly. 'He did tell
me. But I decided I was quite capable of finding New
World on my own.'

'That's not the point. I——'

'Would you mind moving your vehicle?' Frankie asked sweetly. 'We are in rather a hurry. We've a lot of chores to catch up on.'

Mike glared at her for a long moment and at first she thought he was going to be awkward. But then, without another word, he swung round on his heel and marched back to the Land Rover, leaving Frankie feeling illogically let down.

Good heavens, she scolded herself as she engaged first gear and edged past the Land Rover, surely you didn't *want* another confrontation?

It wasn't like Mike to give in so easily, she thought, glancing into her rear-view mirror, expecting to see the Land Rover disappearing down the drive.

But it seemed Mike hadn't given up after all. Instead he had turned his vehicle round and now he was following her, close enough for her to be able to see the frown that drew his dark brows together. Adrenalin coursed through her, her throat tightened and her skin prickled as she increased the pressure on the accelerator, skidding crazily into the farmyard.

She was out of the car and running for the door, leaving two startled boys staring after her. But the moment it took for her to fumble for her keys was her undoing and Mike was upon her.

One hand grasping her elbow, he turned to look at Sid and Tony, who were now standing by the car watching them.

'Get lost, you two,' he ordered, 'find yourselves a job to do.' With that he snatched the keys from Frankie's hand, unlocked the door and thrust her over the threshold. In the kitchen he turned her to face him. 'Right,' he said grimly, 'now you can start explaining.'

'I can't see that I have anything *to* explain,' Frankie retorted, trying not to betray her inner agitation. She tried to ignore the messages her senses were sending her, of his warmth, his aftershave, his very masculine proximity.

'No? How about this, then? Your deliberate discourtesy in going off today to New World, when you knew very well I wanted to take you there myself?' And as she stared mutely at him unable to frame a convincing answer, 'All right, then *I'll* tell *you*. You were running away. Running away from me—but even more importantly, you were running away from yourself—and the way you feel about me.'

He was so right and yet he mustn't know it. Despite the coldness of the day and the fact that she had not yet lit the kitchen fire, prickles of perspiration were breaking out all over her.

'You're talking a load of nonsense,' she said scornfully.

'You know I'm not. And I'm not going to waste time arguing about it.' One large finger traced a lazy path around the contours of her mouth. 'There are far quicker ways of making you admit the truth.'

Although she was warmly clad in jeans and sweater, topped by a shabby coat she had found in her aunt's wardrobe, his gaze seemed to be stripping her of all protection and her face and body were hot with colour as she tried to quell her physical response to him, the knowledge that he was contemplating another of those sensual assaults upon her.

She tried to jerk away but he wouldn't allow it. Holding her fast with one hand, he began to unbutton the coat, sliding it from her shoulders and letting it fall unheeded to the tiled floor.

Then in one swift co-ordinated movement he enfolded her in his arms, at the same time applying the warm, firm pressure of his lips to hers. And Frankie no longer wanted to pull away. Before she knew what she was doing she was responding, her fingers deeply entwined in his hair, as she allowed him to taste and plunder her mouth.

A pervasive lethargy spread throughout her body and she melted pliantly against him. Never had she experienced such immediate surges of physical desire as she did in Mike's arms, an intensity of feeling that obliterated everything else but the desire to be closer, to know the consummation of that desire.

The last coherent thought in her brain before she gave herself up entirely to mindless enjoyment was, That's what it was all about, the fear and the fascination. That's why he always has such an effect on me. I'm in love with him. *This* is what love is really like.

The kiss did not last long enough for Frankie and it was all she could do to stand up, her eyes betraying the depth of her arousal, as he held her away from him. As he surveyed her flushed face a wolfish grin curled his mouth. 'Now try to deny the way you feel about me, Frankie.'

His words jerked her awake but despite the shock she did not take up his challenge. She wanted Mike just as much as he seemed to want her. It was pointless to pretend otherwise when her whole body had just been telling him what he wanted to know.

'What, no argument?' But he didn't sound surprised. He released her and Frankie sank into a chair.

'What's the use?' she said with a rueful little smile.

'Not a lot,' he agreed. He pulled up a chair close to hers and took both of her hands in a strong warm clasp. 'So, now, tell me about New World.'

Frankie stared at him questioningly. She still felt limp with languor, concerned with nothing more at this moment than sorting out her relationship with him. How could he switch so effortlessly to something so mundane? He seemed to read her thoughts.

'Don't worry, Frankie. This is only a breathing-space. In a few moments,' and she shivered at his words, 'I'm going to make love to you very thoroughly. But *after* I've seen the Green boys safely off the premises. We don't want one of their tactless interruptions. Meantime, how about your plans for those unfortunate children?'

'They may be unfortunate in having been born handicapped,' Frankie said slowly, 'but they're certainly fortunate in their surroundings and the people who look after them. It was such a *happy* place, Mike.' As she warmed to her subject her lassitude began to disappear. 'And I really would like to do something for them.' She outlined her conversation with the head-mistress of New World and the momentous decision she had arrived at. 'It means I'll be staying on here after all.' She lifted her chin, daring him to say anything untoward.

'*Well*! When you change your mind you certainly do

it with a vengeance.' Mike's words were teasing but his smile of approbation warmed her.

'You approve of the minibus idea, then?'

'Most definitely. But even more,' his grasp tightened, 'I approve of your staying on here and giving Nigel his marching orders.'

Guilt swept Frankie as she realised how thoroughly she had forgotten Nigel in the last few moments. 'I didn't say anything about that,' she protested.

'Perhaps not, but,' complacently, 'you're going to, aren't you?'

'I. . . I suppose so. But. . .'

'But what, for heaven's sake?' Mike was fierce.

'I. . . I'm not going to. . .to get involved with you until——'

'Involved! What kind of a word is that?' He stood up, hauling her with him. 'You *want* me, Frankie, the way I want you. We already are *involved*, if you must use that word. We——'

'Mike, listen. Let me explain. I mean I'm not going to let you make love to me. I have to see Nigel again. I have to be sure I'm doing the right thing. For all I know this is some sort of madness. Like a holiday romance, born out of unusual surroundings, the fact that you're the only man around. I——'

'What bloody nonsense!' Mike erupted. He shook her, but not ungently. 'Credit yourself with more intelligence than that—and me. You're not on holiday. And *I'm* perfectly sure of my feelings.'

'Maybe you are. But then you're not already engaged. I *have* to be fair to Nigel. I owe him that much. If I'm going to break off with him and marry you, I. . .' She stopped, aware of a sudden new strange tension in Mike that did not stem from his anger. 'What's wrong?' she asked.

His face perfectly expressionless, except perhaps for a hardness in the lines about his mouth, he looked down at her.

'I don't remember,' he said slowly, 'saying anything recently about marriage.'

CHAPTER EIGHT

AT MIKE'S words Frankie's stomach clenched in an intensity of agony. Since she had realised just how she felt about Mike she had hoped he shared her feelings, that it was not just a sexual urge that drew him to her. But now, at the mention of marriage, he seemed to have retreated behind an impenetrable barrier. She felt not only bitterly hurt but embarrassed.

For a long intense moment Frankie held his bleak gaze. Then, slowly, she put up her hands and pushed his from her shoulders. Her throat felt full of tears and she had to swallow before she could speak.

'I see,' she said, turning away from him so he should not see how much he had shocked and hurt her. 'Obviously I misunderstood. I'm sorry. I think you'd better go now, Mike.'

She felt rather than saw his move towards her. 'Frankie, look, let me explain——'

'There's no need. There *is* only one explanation, isn't there? You thought I'd be willing to have an affair with you.' Anger sustained her now as she accused him. 'You actually had the gall to try and break up my engagement for *that*.'

'Frankie,' he put a hand on her arm, 'hold on a moment. You're over-reacting.'

She shrugged him off and turned on him, her eyes cold and hard in a suddenly white face. 'What sort of

149

reaction did you expect? Gratitude?' As he reached out once more, 'Don't touch me! Don't ever touch me again. Get out of this house!' Her voice rose unevenly. 'Get out! Do you hear me?'

As he parted his lips to speak once more there was a knock on the door and Frankie flew to answer it.

'Good grief, Frankie! Talk about the back of beyond!'

'Nigel!'

He stood there, slight and blond and handsome, and she thought she had never been so glad to see anyone in her life. With a muffled sob she flung herself into his arms. And because Mike had just shattered a fragile fledgeling dream, she was more affectionate in her greeting than she might have been. 'Oh, Nigel, you've come at last!'

Nigel, accepting her effusive welcome as his due, steered her back into the room. 'I heard raised voices,' he said with a suspicious look at Mike. 'This fellow giving you trouble?'

She dared not look at Mike. 'N-nothing I can't handle. He. . . he was just leaving anyway.'

'On your way, then, mate!' Nigel jerked his head towards the still-open door.

Despite her distress Frankie could not help thinking how ludicrous the situation was. If Mike decided he did not want to go there was no way Nigel could make him. Poor Nigel, she thought with a pang of guilty compassion, he was no competition for Mike with his virile authority and strength. It would be David and Goliath all over again. But this time Goliath would be the victor.

She had made much of Nigel deliberately. But, that done, she knew with a dreadful certainty that he could not hold a candle to Mike where she was concerned. Nigel might be more beautiful to look at, but he was pale cold moonlight to Mike's rugged warmth. Mike's warmth! Which would never be hers.

She turned away, her back towards the two men as she fought for control. She did not want either of them to see how upset she was. Then she heard the back door close with a quietness that was more final than if it had been slammed—and she knew with wrenching pain that Mike had gone.

Fighting for composure, she took a deep breath and turned back towards Nigel. He was not looking at her. Instead he was making a comprehensive study of the kitchen and she could tell at once that he did not like what he saw.

'What a dump! And I had a hell of a job finding this place. It's the absolute pits. And that driveway—lord knows what it's done to my springs. I've shoved the car in that barn thing, by the way.' And now at last he did move towards her, bestowing a perfunctory kiss on her cheek. 'Well, now I'm here we'll soon have this business sorted out and get you back to civilisation. Who *was* that fellow, by the way? Disreputable-looking type. A farmhand, I suppose?'

'That was Mike. Mike Leeming.'

'The trustee fellow?' Nigel stared his incredulity. 'Good lord. Your aunt actually entrusted her affairs to a roughneck like that? She must have been barmy. Dammit. If I'd known who he was I wouldn't have got rid of him so smartly. What were you quarrelling about? I suppose he's still being obstructive about handing over to you?'

Frankie was discovering something. That it was all right for her to criticise and lambast Mike, but that it was very far from all right to stand and listen to someone else doing so. She sprang to Mike's defence.

'No, he's not being obstructive. Oh, we didn't get on too well at first. But that was a misunderstanding. He's been a great help. And he's not a roughneck. It's no good a vet wearing his best clothes to work. And. . .and I'd just told him I'd decided to stay here after all.'

Nigel nodded complacently. 'Just a bluff, of course, as I suggested. But he didn't like it, huh? Just shows he's out to get your aunt's money into his own hands. Well, there's no need for you to bury yourself alive. There has to be some way to sort out this legacy of yours.'

'Nigel, please, sit down for a minute and listen. A lot's happened since I last spoke to you. I've changed my mind. I *want* to stay here. No, hear me out.' For the moment, as she outlined her ideas for Lionswick Farm and the sanctuary, she managed to shake off the anguish Mike had caused her.

Nigel did hear her out, though she could tell by the growing look of displeasure on his face, his irritated gestures, that there was no way he would ever have agreed to her plans. That didn't matter now, of course, but sure enough, the moment she was silent, he exploded into speech.

'You've obviously taken leave of your senses. Otherwise how the hell could you imagine I'd agree to bury myself out here? You know being near London is important to me—and being near my mother too. She *needs* me.'

Frankie gave him a long, considering look, taking in the furrowed brow below floppy fair hair, the petulant twist of his mouth. She realised that he hadn't said he'd missed her. Instead he had launched into a diatribe—against the countryside, the house, Mike—even against her and her plans.

It had taken these two weeks apart from him to show her just how self-centred Nigel was—and she didn't count his consideration for his mother. She was beginning to see that this too smacked of self-interest. Being the apple of his mother's eye *suited* Nigel. *He* didn't want that to change. Besides, now a whole host of recollections flooded back, of times when she had given way to him, just to keep the peace.

'I've told you before, Nigel, there's no way I'd agree to live with—or even too near—your mother. I——'

'Frankie!' Slumped at the kitchen table, the look of dissatisfaction marring his handsome features, he said, 'Forget all that nonsense for a minute, because it *is* nonsense—I'll decide where we're going to live. Even with your legacy we couldn't afford to buy a place and I'm not renting, putting money in landlords' pockets. Look, I'm hungry. Aren't you going to offer me a meal?'

'Heavens!' Frankie clapped a hand to her mouth. Sid's and Tony's breakfast had cleaned out her small store of food. 'I'm afraid I can't. What with one thing and another, I forgot to do some shopping today.'

'You mean you've no food in the house at all?' Nigel

looked even more aggrieved. 'I drive all this way and——'

'If you'd let me know you were coming,' Frankie began, and then, 'but there's no point in arguing about it. The best thing is for one of us to go down to the village. There's a fish and chip shop——'

'*Fish and chips*?'

Anyone would think she'd offered him arsenic on toast, Frankie thought. But then Nigel had always been fussy about his food. She blamed his mother for that. Children needed to experience a wide range of tastes. Nigel had probably never eaten fish and chips in the whole of his spoilt life. He would never try foreign cuisine either.

'None of your Italian or Chinese muck for me,' he had said once when Frankie suggested a change of menu.

Frankie loved trying new and exotic dishes and had consoled herself by eating them on days when she was not seeing Nigel, in case a whiff of some exotic spice incurred his fastidious disapproval. But, she thought with satisfaction, she didn't have to consult his tastes any more.

'I'm afraid it's that or nothing,' she told him now, remembering wistfully how she and Mike had relished their fish and chip supper.

Mike! Suddenly the pain was back—had never really left her. She had been so certain that Mike had had marriage in mind when he'd urged her to break with Nigel. And now that it was an impossibility, she knew she had wanted that more than anything else in the world—to be with Mike, to share his life, to have *him* share *hers*. His work and that of the sanctuary would have dovetailed together so well. And she had believed they were equally compatible.

Nigel's voice interrupted this train of thought. 'Well, if there's no food I might as well go to bed. I'm dog-tired as well. *Now* what's wrong?' as Frankie's too-expressive face betrayed her.

'I. . . I'm afraid there isn't a spare bed. My. . .my aunt hadn't bothered to furnish the other rooms. But there's a couch in the living-room.'

'Damn that for a lark. I'm used to a proper bed. I'll share yours.'

'No, you won't!'

'Frankie, for Pete's sake, what's the matter with that? I've been pretty restrained these last few months. But I'm only human. We'll be getting married in a few weeks' time. Now that you've come into money there's no reason to——'

'Nigel!' She was exasperated. 'I don't believe you've understood a word I've said. If I don't stay here and look after the place there won't *be* any money. And all right, *you* can have the bed. *I'll* sleep on the couch. But surely you're not going up yet?' she said as Nigel immediately rose. 'We've. . .we've got to talk. I——'

'Not tonight, Frankie.' He yawned vastly. 'I'm tired, I'm hungry—and cold. This house is like an igloo. Isn't there any damned heating either?'

'I'll give you my hot-water bottle as well!' Frankie snapped.

When Nigel had gone upstairs, she sat on alone in the kitchen, taking stock of the events of the past hour. It was a lot to assimilate. That hour had seen the realisation of her love for Mike. It had also seen a dawning dream brutally shattered.

For a moment of bitter chagrin, when Mike had disclaimed any thoughts of marriage, Frankie had believed she could—that she *must*—root out this new love from her heart. She had even believed that she could go ahead and marry Nigel as planned. But the last hour had also revealed the impossibility of that. The moment she had seen him and Mike together she had known.

How had she ever believed she was in love with Nigel? Anything she had ever felt for him had been a pale imitation of the real thing. And looking back she knew what she'd felt for him had not even been born out of love. She had chosen to marry Nigel because he represented an unthreatening relationship, no highs, no lows, no risks. With his steady unadventurous lifestyle, he had promised her a security her mother had never known.

Frankie supposed she had always known that, despite her father's faults, her mother had gone on loving him, right up until the end of her life, long after he had reduced them to poverty and ended his own life ignominiously by falling, when drunk, under the wheels of a lorry.

It had taken her meeting with Mike to show her that love without security might not be the ideal, but then neither was *security* without *love*.

It wasn't going to be a pleasant task, but tomorrow she would have to tell Nigel what she had wanted to tell him tonight, that she couldn't marry him. And now it wasn't just because of Mike. Since it seemed she wouldn't be marrying him either. She might very well, she thought with an aching heart, end up as an eccentric old spinster like Aunt Francesca. But that would be infinitely better than living a lie.

On that thought she went to her makeshift bed on the couch. She was sure Mike would never have deprived her of her bed. But she must *stop* thinking about Mike. Her new life was not, after all, going to include him.

Despite the discomforts she slept surprisingly well. And she was up early to tidy the bedclothes away out of the living-room. But she was still in dressing-gown and slippers, making the first cup of tea of the day, when Sid and Tony arrived.

To her surprise Mike was with them and what was more all three seemed to be on extremely friendly terms.

Mike, for the first time since she'd known him, was dressed formally in a dark suit and crisp white shirt. At the sight of him the familiar weakness filled her body, beginning as tension low in her stomach then invading her veins, turning her muscles to jelly, leaving her rooted to the spot. Why was he here?

'I thought it was only fair,' he said, a hand on each boy's shoulder, 'since I mentioned it to you in the first place—to tell you that these two have been completely exonerated.'

Frankie stared at him blankly, registering nothing of what he was saying. She was still trying to cope with her reactions at seeing him. Suddenly she was wondering if she *could* go on living here, in the circumstances.

Seeing Mike whenever his veterinary services were required would only be a frustratingly painful reminder of her feelings for him and the painful knowledge that his desire for her had been just that—a physical wanting, not a total commitment of himself.

'Frankie!' He moved closer and snapped a finger and thumb before her glazed eyes. 'You look still half asleep.' For the first time he seemed to notice what she was wearing. Sharply, 'Are you all right? Have you only just got up?'

'Er—yes. I——'

He moved closer and turned her face up to the light, and at the touch of his fingers Frankie had to repress a shudder of pure sensuality. 'You look tired. What time did Greaves go last night?'

'He didn't. He——'

Mike's hand fell away abruptly. 'You mean he spent the night here?'

'Well. . .yes. What's wrong with——?

His face was grim. 'Only that I happen to know there's only one bed in this house. You told me you'd never slept with Greaves. Why did you do it, Frankie? Just to spite me?'

Frankie flared up immediately. 'Don't flatter yourself, Mike Leeming. When I sleep with someone it will be because *I* want to, not for any other reason. And for your information I did *not* sleep with Nigel. I slept on the couch.'

Without a word he turned on his heel and marched through to the living-room. Frankie, who knew what he would find—or rather what he would *not* find— waited resignedly.

With half her attention on the receding sound of his footsteps, she turned to the two boys. She felt uncomfortable that they had been witnesses to this exchange. 'What did he mean—about you? Being exonerated?'

Sid, as always, was the one to reply. 'Folks in the village 'ad given us a bad name. They thought we'd been the ones nickin' from shops. But they've found out it were the postmistress's son. So Mr Leeming, 'e said it were only fair he should tell you he 'ad no objection now to us workin' 'ere.'

'Big of him!' Frankie said sarcastically. 'Considering he had no say in it anyway. Look, Sid, could you and Tony let the donkeys out into their paddocks and we'll feed them there, the way we did before, after Mr Leeming's gone?'

She had heard Mike coming back, and when he re-entered the kitchen she saw at once that he was in one of his black moods and his dark eyes as he looked at her were full of scorn.

'I cleared the blankets away as soon as I got up,' she forestalled him by saying.

'Save your breath!' He made for the back door and once more Frankie lost her temper, really lost it this time. She wasn't sure which was making her the angriest. How dared he question her private life? How dared he make love to her, try to break up her relationship with Nigel without any honourable intentions on his own part? How dared he accuse her of lying?

She flew at him, grabbing him by both arms, exerting all her strength to shake him. She might as well have assaulted a monolith. He remained as immovable.

'*I do not tell lies*!' she shouted at him. 'OK, so I can't prove I didn't sleep with Nigel, but what damned business is it of yours if I did? *You* have no claims on me. You waived all rights to any say in my life, yesterday. You. . .you sanctimonious hypocrite. You act outraged because you think I was with Nigel last night. But what was it *you* were wanting me to do?' When he did not answer, she stamped her foot. 'Answer me, damn you. What makes it wrong to go to bed with him and right to go to bed with you?'

The violence of her movements had loosened the belt of her dressing-gown and the nightdress beneath was not proof against his suddenly arrested eyes. Angrily aware of exposed creamy flesh, she snatched the lapels together.

'You can take your. . .your lust elsewhere, Mike Leeming. I didn't get a chance to tell you, but I'm glad I misunderstood. It's a good thing you don't want to marry me. It saves me having to deflate your ego. I wouldn't want to marry you either, do you hear?'

If he had been angry before he was doubly so now. Hard hands grasped her shoulders. He looked as if *he* would like to shake *her*. But he did not, for which Frankie was eternally grateful. If he had she might have burst into tears. As it was, now her own rage was spent, she had to bite hard on her lower lip to still its threatened quivering.

'Don't act the shrew, Frankie,' he said quietly. 'It doesn't suit you. As it happens there are a lot of things *I* didn't get a chance to tell *you*. We were interrupted by Greaves's arrival, if you remember? I know you were angry with me yesterday, and hurt. But,' bitterly, 'you're not in love with him. So wasn't it rather a pointless gesture to sleep with him? I mean, I would never have known if I hadn't walked in this morning. Or did you plan to tell me?'

She stared at him incredulously. 'I just don't believe what I'm hearing,' she said after a while. 'You've really managed to convince yourself, haven't you?' The evaporation of her anger left her drained and depressed. If Mike could believe something like that of her, there was no hope for. . . But there was no hope anyway, she reminded herself. She shrugged helplessly. 'Oh, think what you like, damn you. I'm sick and tired of arguing with you. I'm sick and tired of *you*!'

As she spoke his hands had dropped to his side and now he moved away. He spoke coldly. 'I see. In that case it's just as well I have an appointment to keep. Because *I* don't feel much like arguing either. I came here this morning intending to. . . Oh, what's the use?' He moved to the door, turning to deliver his parting shot. 'I shall be away for a few days. But if you need a vet, ring the usual number. I've got a locum in.'

As the door slammed behind him, Frankie groped blindly for a chair. But she was not allowed any privacy to cope with the tears that slid down her face. As she heard Nigel coming downstairs she moved hastily to the sink, pretending to be engrossed in washing her cup.

'What the hell was all that shouting about?' Nigel came yawning into the kitchen.

She dashed a hand over her eyes and turned to look at him. His hair was dishevelled, his eyes still heavy.

Blond stubble blurred the edges of his face, emphasising the beginning of a double chin. Nigel was putting on weight. But of course his mother overfed him and he never took any real exercise. It was the first time Frankie had seen him at this time of day. Everyone, she thought through her misery, should have an opportunity of seeing their future partner at their worst. If love could survive that. . .

But Nigel wasn't her future partner any more. She didn't love him. But she did love Mike, in spite of having seen him tired, scruffy and dishevelled. Again she brushed the sleeve of her dressing-gown across her eyes.

'You've been crying,' Nigel observed. Mike would have come to her and put an arm around her. Nigel did not. He had once said he couldn't stand women who were always weeping. Then, 'That shouting? Was it that Leeming fellow here again? Where does he hang out? I'll see him today and give him a piece of my mind.'

'You'll do no such thing!' Frankie snapped. It was such a relief to be able to disagree openly with Nigel. So often in the past she had demurred to him. But in the past few days she had been making her own decisions and discovering that she enjoyed it. 'I'm going to get dressed,' she told him. 'And you'd better do the same. We have to talk. But first I have to help the boys feed the donkeys.'

'Boys? What boys?'

'Sid and Tony, from the village. I did mention them last night, when I explained my plans for this place.'

Half an hour later she re-entered the kitchen, to find

Nigel sitting at the table, his hands clasped around a mug of coffee.

'What's the ghastly smell in here?' he demanded. 'It was even wafting up the stairs.'

'Bran, for the donkeys.'

'You prepare it here? In the same kitchen you use for your own food?'

'At the moment, yes. All that will change eventually.' She brushed the subject aside and took the chair facing him. 'Nigel, I'm sorry, but there's no easy way to say this, so I'm going to come straight to the point. I'm not going to marry you.'

His face ludicrous with surprise, he stared at her. 'Why?' he demanded.

'Because I've realised I'm not in love with you I thought I was. But I'm not. I'm sorry,' she said again.

As she watched, his expression changed, hardened, became accusing. 'You don't have to tell me why. I can guess. There's someone else, isn't there? Is it that Leeming fellow? Have you been carrying on with him since you've been here?'

It was close enough to the truth to make Frankie colour up. But, 'I've done nothing I'm ashamed of,' she said. 'It's just that this separation from you has given me a chance to look at. . .at *us*. And realise that it just wouldn't work. I can't be the sort of person you want me to be. I'm not even the person *I* thought I was. I'm not coming back to London, Nigel. I'm going to stay here and do what my aunt wanted me to do.'

'And marry Leeming, I suppose? You! Married to a local yokel? You wouldn't last five minutes. You're a city girl.'

'I'm not, actually. Not really. And Mike is *not* a yokel! He's an intelligent, educated man. He just happens to be the local veterinary surgeon. And anyway,' she could not keep the despondency out of her voice, 'I'm not going to marry him. He hasn't asked me.'

'But you fancy him!' Nigel said. He stood up. His face was white and angry and Frankie felt a pang of guilt at the thought of how hurt he must feel. But not for long. For it seemed Nigel's pride was more injured than his heart. 'Well, I can't help thinking it's probably all for the best. I've had my own doubts. But I kept telling myself it would be different when we were married. That you and mother would come to love each other. But you've never really tried to get along with her, have you? I find that very hurtful and so does she.'

For just one blinding second of fury, Frankie felt like telling him just what she thought of his mother, telling him how obstructive and uncooperative Mrs Greaves had always been. She *knew* Mrs Greaves had been against their marriage right from the start. But what was the point? It would only seem like vindictiveness. Let Nigel keep his illusions. He would find out for himself some time. Or maybe he'd find someone else who would tolerate the strings which kept him bound to his mother.

It was a relief when Nigel had taken his overnight bag and departed. But the relief was short-lived. She was alone here now, totally alone. She had cut the last tie with her former life and committed herself to this solitary existence, her only company the donkeys and a couple of cows.

'Miss! Miss!' She had forgotten Sid and Tony and she was suddenly grateful for their presence.

'I think,' she said, 'it's about time you started calling me Frankie. But what's all the excitement?' For Sid's freckled face was pale and anxious and his eyes glittered with some strong emotion. Even the normally stolid Tony seemed unusually animated.

'We been looking round those outbuildings, like what you told us. To see what needed doin' to turn 'em into cages and runs and suchlike. Miss—Frankie. . .did you know, there's a flat up above them stables? Me and Tony, we could fix it up. We could live there. It'd be our very own place. Get us out of Mum's hair. O' course, we'd pay rent,' he added hastily. 'Oh, Miss—Frankie. . .can we?'

'I'd better come and have a look,' Frankie said slowly.

Why not, if the place was suitable? she thought as she followed Sid and Tony across the yard. It could be the ideal solution to her isolation. At least it would mean another human presence about the place.

It was obvious that the flat had not been used for some time, probably not during her aunt's ownership of the farm. But it had possibilities. The basic essentials were there.

'We'd clean it up and decorate, wouldn't we, Tone?' Sid's eyes had been fixed anxiously on Frankie's face as they toured the three rooms the flat boasted. Kitchenette, a large bed-sitting room and a minute bathroom.

'It's a bit small for two,' Frankie said doubtfully. But

then, remembering the even more cramped accommodation the boys presently occupied, she relented. 'But only if your mother says you may,' she warned. 'She may not like you leaving home.'

She did not sleep at all that night. Infuriatingly, she lay awake brooding over Mike Leeming and his despicable behaviour. It was the first time she had ever lost any sleep over a man. Nigel had never aroused such strong emotions in her, emotions composed of inextricably mixed longing and anger.

Next morning the second of the pregnant mares decided to go into labour. It was Sid who brought her the news and it only took one brief look for Frankie to know that this birth too was going to be a difficult one—and Mike was away somewhere. Again she wondered where he had gone.

She ran back to the house and dialled the surgery number. 'Oh, Mrs Leeming,' she said with relief. 'is Mike's locum there? Will you tell him it's urgent?'

She waited barely long enough for Mrs Leeming's reassuring reply before returning to the stable. So when the vet did arrive it was a surprise to find the locum was female.

'Deborah Barker,' the other woman introduced herself. 'Now, let's see what we have here.'

She didn't look like a veterinary surgeon, was Frankie's first thought. Tall and slender, she looked far too elegant ever to get her hands soiled. But Frankie was soon revising her opinion, as Deborah dealt with the breech presentation as efficiently as Mike had done, keeping up a running conversation as she did so.

'I've been here once or twice before, in the old lady's time. She tolerated me but it was obvious I couldn't hold a candle to Mike in her eyes. I think she looked on him as the son she never had. Certainly she was as indignant as any mother could be when his wife walked out on him.'

'Wife?' Frankie said sharply. 'I didn't know Mike was married.'

Deborah Barker looked keenly at her for a moment. 'Oh, yes,' she said drily, 'very much so. I fancied Mike myself when I first came here—and I let him see it, I'm afraid. But he was the faithful type. Some men are like that, aren't they? Once in love, always in love.'

'You said his wife walked out on him?'

'Yes. She wasn't really suited to this sort of life. I gather she was a model—with a well-known London fashion house, I believe. Goodness knows how Mike met her. Anyway, she stuck this place for a couple of years, then one day she just upped and left—went back to the fashion world, I presume. I don't think he's ever recovered.'

No wonder Mike had been so scathing about *her* career, Frankie thought. In his eyes there was probably very little difference between a fashion and a photographic model. No wonder he'd said 'young women these days seem incapable of sustained effort'.

'I take it there weren't any children?' she asked. She felt a little uncomfortable, quizzing Mike's locum about him. But she couldn't ask someone else.

'No, fortunately.'

'I suppose. . . I suppose they *are* divorced?' Mike had definitely told her he had no wife. She did not like to think he might have lied to her. Why, he had even proposed to her once. But, as she had suspected at the time, that must have been a bad joke.

Again the other's shrewd eyes raked Frankie's face. 'Keen on him yourself, are you? Well, good luck, dear, but I think you're on a losing wicket. As to divorce, I'm afraid I don't know. I'm not a local, do you see? This is the first time Mike's called me in for ages. He's not often away.'

She put the foal to the mare to suckle and stood up. 'There, he'll do. Well-made little chap. I'll look back tomorrow. But if you're worried at all before then, give me a call.'

Thank goodness for Sid and Tony and their affairs to keep her occupied. Sid had not wasted a moment in obtaining his mother's agreement to his and Tony's moving into the stableyard flat; and somehow Frankie found herself inveigled into driving him into town to buy decorating materials. 'So long as you do it on your own time,' she warned him.

Between that and her regular chores, she was kept busy all day with no time to sit and ponder over what she had learned.

But when evening came it was a different matter. Sid and Tony had gone home, the animals were all settled for the night. Peace engulfed the farmhouse. But there was no peace in Frankie's heart.

While she had believed Mike to be single there had always been the secret hope that his physical need of her would lead eventually to his falling in love with her and bring him round to the idea of marriage. But now, for all she knew he had lied to her. He might still be married and—if Deborah was a reliable informant—he was probably still in love with his wife.

She had to know the truth, Frankie decided, just as another sleepless dawn was breaking. And, she realised, there *was* one person who could tell her about Mike—his mother.

CHAPTER NINE

'FRANKIE! How lovely to see you!' There was no mistaking the warmth of Mrs Leeming's welcome. 'I'm so glad you've come today because as soon as Mike gets back I'm off home. The decorators have finished at long last, thank goodness.'

Frankie had wondered how she was going to excuse her impromptu visit but Mrs Leeming did not seem to find it strange that she should just call in. All she had to do now was to casually lead the conversation round to Mike and hope his mother would fill in the information she needed.

'He looked very smart the other day,' she said as she followed Mrs Leeming into the kitchen. 'It's the first time I've ever seen him in a suit.'

'He's not a great one for dressing up,' Mrs Leeming agreed, 'but even he couldn't go up to London in his working clothes.'

London! His wife had gone back to London. With an effort she kept her voice steady. 'A week or two ago I would have envied him,' she said. 'But not any more. I've decided to stay here after all—to live here, I mean.'

Mrs Leeming looked surprised. 'I didn't realise there was any question of your *not* staying, my dear.'

'You mean Mike didn't tell you? About the awful

rows we had when I first arrived? Because I said there was no way I would stay and run the sanctuary.'

'Heavens, no! Mike's not like that. He's a very loyal person. Why, I didn't even know there was trouble between him and Liz until it was too late.'

Frankie's heart skipped a beat. Here it came. It was almost too easy. 'Liz?' she said enquiringly.

'His wife. Or rather, his ex-wife, I should say.'

So he *was* divorced. Relief swept through Frankie's entire body and she relaxed back into her chair. 'He's never mentioned her,' she told Mrs Leeming.

'No, well, he wouldn't. As I said, he's very loyal. If he can't say anything good about anyone he doesn't mention them at all. Some of these old village biddies could do with taking a leaf out of his book.'

Mrs Leeming had heard about *her* before they met, Frankie thought. So that must mean he couldn't have disapproved of her altogether. Then another thought occurred to her. 'But he told me about Sid and Tony Green?'

'Only for your protection,' Mrs Leeming said hastily. 'And you will admit he was quick to set the record straight. And he's never said anything unkind about *you*. When he brought you here to dinner I did think perhaps. . . But maybe I was wrong.'

Infuriatingly she said no more on that subject. Instead she poured two mugs of coffee and suggested to Frankie that they take them into the living-room. 'I wasn't in England when Mike and Liz split up,' she said as they sat down. 'Something I very much regretted. I have a cousin in Canada and she'd been pressing me for years to pay her a long visit. It all flared up during those six months.'

'How long ago was that?'

'Getting on for two years. It's been a very lonely two years for him. I've kept hoping he'd eventually meet someone else. But there's not much opportunity here in Lionswick. Besides, it's not as if he and Liz stopped loving each other. She just couldn't stand country life. She missed her career, the bright lights. Mike goes up to London about once a month to see her. I suppose he lives in hope of persuading her to come back. Perhaps he thinks her career will pall one day.'

Or that she'll lose her looks, Frankie thought ironically, remembering his words to her.

'So that's where he's gone this week,' Mrs Leeming added, unnecessarily for Frankie. 'To see Liz.'

Frankie was glad when Mrs Leeming chattered on over a seemingly endless range of subjects. For she felt totally incapable of keeping up her end of the conversation. She had come here to learn what she could about Mike and she had found out plenty. But there was no pleasure, only heartache, in the discoveries she had made. Mike had gone to London, to see the wife he still loved and who still loved him. Did they still go to bed together, she wondered painfully, on these visits to London?

'I'll be glad to get back to my friends and my bridge club and my own cosy little place,' Mrs Leeming was confessing. 'I love Mike dearly and this was my home once. But I find it too large and rambling these days. There's not much social life. And we haven't seen the worst of the winter yet. Once or twice this last week

I've thought it was cold enough for snow. I should keep plenty of provisions in if I were you, dear. In case you get snowed up out at the farm.'

Frankie stayed long enough for courtesy but it was difficult to hide her depression and it was a relief when she could finally get away from Mrs Leeming's well-meaning advice.

It was a pity she had not heeded that advice. For she woke up next morning to a white world of drifts, cutting her off not only from the outside world but even from the village—and she had only bought enough food for one day.

Under normal circumstances she would have thought the snow beautiful, but today she looked at it with a jaundiced eye. Not only would it make her trek to the stables more difficult, but the donkeys would have to be kept in.

There was no time for breakfast. Something had to be done about her situation.

The snow in the yard was wellington-high. How on earth was she going to walk, let alone carry the heavy buckets? What a pity Sid and Tony were not yet in residence.

An examination of her resources revealed nothing more useful than a spade. She would have to dig her way out.

Easier said than done. Half an hour later she had only succeeded in making an eighteen-inch-wide track half-way across the yard.

The change in the weather had not affected the donkeys' appetites, she thought as she paused for a rest. They were bawling their heads off as though in the terminal stages of starvation.

'Oh, shut up!' Frankie muttered crossly. She was more concerned about Daisy and Blossom, whom she could hear persistently lowing from the barn. Milking time was well overdue.

She carried on digging, but more slowly; her first energetic efforts had tired her. Inside her weatherproof clothing the sweat trickled down her back and between her breasts. She felt slightly dizzy.

'Hello, there!' a distant shout assailed her.

At first Frankie thought she was hallucinating, so much was Mike on her mind these days. For it had sounded like his voice. But when she turned around there was no sign of the Land Rover. Not even that sturdy vehicle could have made it up here in these conditions.

'Frankie!' It came from right behind her and she swung round violently, nearly falling over as she did so.

A strong hand caught and supported her.

'Mike! How on earth did you——?' But a glance at his feet told her everything. He was wearing skis.

He grinned. 'A useful accomplishment, isn't it, for a country vet? This won't be the first time I've had to rescue some beleaguered Cotsaller.' Despite the weather he seemed to be in a much sunnier mood than at their last encounter and Frankie, never one to bear a grudge, responded.

'Well, I'm glad you've come to *my* rescue this time,' she admitted. 'Though more for the animals' sake,' she added hastily, 'than for my own. They're making the most dreadful hullabaloo.'

Mike discarded his skis and took the spade from her unresisting hand. 'You get the kettle on,' he told her. 'You look as though you could do with a break. And I'll need reviving myself after this little lot.' He began to dig with large sweeping strokes, clearing more in one spadeful than Frankie had been able to shift in three. Thankfully she left him to it.

As she waited for the kettle to boil, she couldn't help wondering why he had chosen to come to *her* assistance. There must be many people in and around Lionswick, snowed in, who would have been glad of his services this morning.

'What's happening about your surgery?' she asked him when he came in ten minutes later and held out his hand for the warming coffee.

'Deborah's seeing to that. She was here for a week anyway. And I came home sooner than planned.'

Frankie longed to know why. It was true, the old saying, she thought—'Hope springs eternal'. Perhaps his visit to his ex-wife this time had not been a success.

But there was no time for speculation. After gulping down his coffee in record time, without even bothering to sit down, Mike began to organise things.

'I'll see to the feeding of the five thousand,' he quipped, 'if you'll milk Daisy and Blossom. Once the animals are seen to we'll have time for ourselves.'

And what did that mean? Frankie wondered.

Milking, as a rule, was a soothing occupation. The rhythmic movements, the warm sweet smell of the cows' breath. But this morning her hands seemed unusually shaky, her movements uncoordinated.

She had just finished her task when Mike appeared to help carry the pails of milk back to the house.

'Watch your step,' he warned her. 'It's still freezing. It's slippy underfoot.'

Back in the kitchen, the emergency over, Frankie found herself tongue-tied. But Mike did not seem to have a similar problem as he set about lighting the fire.

'One of your first jobs, now you're staying, will be to get central heating installed,' he told her.

'I suppose so,' Frankie said vaguely. She did not seem able to concentrate on anything. She watched Mike as he knelt at the fireplace. Hungrily she studied every line of him, the broad back, the strong nape of his neck where the black hair, in need of a cut, curled thickly, tempting her fingers.

Her chest was filled with a breathless panicky feeling and her stomach churned. He would be leaving soon. She could scarcely expect him to stay now that he had done what he could to help. She wished desperately that there was something she could say or do to keep him here—just a little longer.

As he stood up and turned to face her, all her doubts and fears engulfed her. She felt her head swim and she must have swayed visibly, because he crossed the kitchen in a couple of strides and grasped her by the elbows. 'Frankie? What is it? You're as white as a sheet. You look as though you're about to pass out.' Then, suspiciously, 'Have you eaten this morning?'

She shook her head. 'Not yet. I had to get to the animals.'

Mike pulled out one of the kitchen chairs and firmly thrust her into it. With the ease of long familiarity, he put out the necessary utensils and soon the smell of frying bacon and eggs filled the kitchen. In the grate the fire crackled encouragingly and suddenly the world did not seem quite so bleak after all.

'Mike——' Frankie began.

'Eat that!' He put a heaped plate in front of her and began to attack his own. 'There'll be plenty of time to talk afterwards.'

So he wasn't going to leave her immediately. Frankie ate with a better appetite than she had expected.

At last, replete, she pushed back her chair and carried her empty plate to the sink.

'Leave the washing up for now,' Mike ordered brusquely. 'Sit down again. There's something I have to say to you.'

Mutely, she obeyed him, her eyes large in her still-pale face.

'First off,' he went on after an agonisingly long silence, 'I reckon I owe you an apology. I shouldn't have doubted your word the other morning.'

'No, you shouldn't have,' Frankie muttered. But he went on as if she hadn't spoken.

'I think I know you well enough by now to know that you're not petty or spiteful. You have too much integrity to make use of a man you don't love any more, just to score a point.'

He leaned forward across the table, his dark grey eyes earnest. 'I can only excuse myself by saying I was under a certain amount of stress that morning. It made me act like an idiot. Will you forgive me, Frankie?' He held out his hand.

Tremulously Frankie put her fingers into his strong warm clasp. It was exquisite torture to feel his flesh enclosing hers once more.

He did not release her hand but closed both of his around it. 'There's something I have to explain to you. It concerns the way I've been behaving lately—and the physical attraction I feel towards you.'

'Please, Mike, don't.' She tried to withdraw her hand but he would not relinquish it. She did not want to hear him explain about Liz and so she tried to forestall him. 'I know that you were married and that——'

'And that I'm divorced,' he said, regaining the initiative. 'Do you disapprove of divorce, Frankie? I mean, do you have any strong religious grounds for condemning it?'

She shook her head, her eyes still fixed on their clasped hands. She didn't know where this conversation was leading. She was not sure she was even up to an intellectual discussion. Her brain felt fogged, all sensation was concentrated in her body, which throbbed to the contact transmitted through their entwined fingers.

'When Liz left me,' Mike went on slowly, 'my world was torn apart. She was—*is* the most beautiful woman I've ever met.'

And he didn't even say 'present company excepted', Frankie thought. It would have been a matter for self-deprecatory laughter if she had not been so close to tears.

'When I met Liz and married her, I couldn't believe

my good fortune—that such a gorgeous creature should be as besotted with me as I was with her. Our honeymoon was bliss—and so were the first few months of our marriage.'

I don't want to hear this, Frankie thought desperately, her green eyes unconsciously pleading with him to spare her. She didn't want to know the intimate details. The thought of Mike making love to another woman was unbearable. But he was still speaking and as he did so his forefinger idly traced a mesmeric pattern on the veins in Frankie's wrist.

'But I should have known it was too good to last. I was like a miser, hiding his treasure in a cobweb-filled attic. Liz wasn't the type for obscurity. In town and in her career she had blossomed. In the country she faded. The rows began and then. . . Oh, well, to cut a long story short, she left me. But before she went she tried to persuade me to go with her, to get a town practice. She still loved me, you see, in spite of everything.'

There was a long silence, during which Frankie's heart ached—for him—and for herself. 'Did you not even consider it?' she asked at last.

He nodded. 'But I knew it wouldn't work out. Aside from the fact that I'd taken over my father's practice, I'm no more a townee than Liz was a countrywoman. It would have been better if we'd never met.'

'You still see her, don't you?' Frankie said, the words coming from between painfully stiff dry lips. She wasn't sure how much more of this she could take. Every instinct longed to go round the table to him and cradle his dark head against her breast, to tell him that if he would only love her, *she* would never leave him.

Fool, she berated herself. To think that *you* could ever erase the memory of the most beautiful woman he'd ever known.

'Yes. In the last two years I've seen her, regularly, once a month. Your aunt had a hand in that. I told you I owed her a lot.'

'Aunt Francesca?' For a moment Frankie was surprised out of her despair.

'Mmm. She was the only person I could bring myself to talk to. After Liz left I was totally devastated. My initial reaction—pride speaking, of course—was to have a clean break. To hell with Liz—to hell with all women.'

'And Auntie Fran advised against it?' Oh, Auntie! Frankie thought reproachfully. If you hadn't done that, by now he might have been over her, free to love again.

'She was a wise old bird, your aunt. She may never have been married but she knew a lot about love. She contended that if our love was meant to be, Liz and I would eventually get back together again. Keep the channels open, she said.'

Frankie was very much afraid she was going to be sick. Suddenly her breakfast lay too heavily in her stomach. She knew what was coming next. He was going to tell her that her wise aunt had been right— that he and his wife were reconciled.

'When I saw Liz this week, we had a long chat. Perhaps the frankest discussion we've ever had. We were able for perhaps the first time to look at ourselves and our relationship logically, without physicality blurring the outlines. And we came to an agreement.'

Frankie bowed her head, so that he should not see

she had closed her eyes tightly. She swallowed, fighting back the nausea that threatened to overwhelm her. Let it be over soon, she prayed. Make him cut it short, finish and then go, so I can be alone with my misery, so I can save some remnants of my pride.

'I told you I was under stress the other day. It was because I was going to see Liz and because of what I had to say to her. I had to ask her if she was still in love with me. I didn't want to hurt her, you see.'

Silence. Frankie dared not open her eyes to look at him. Her eyelids, so tightly squeezed shut, were only just succeeding in holding back the tears.

'Frankie.' His voice was exultant now and she braced herself for the blow that must fall. 'She doesn't love me any more. There's someone else. *She* was afraid at first to tell *me*. Frankie, I'm free—I'm finally free.'

She did look at him then, puzzled, incredulous at his jubilation. And now the tears fell, thick and fast, cascading down her cheeks.

'I. . . I'm sorry.' She used her free hand to dash them away and essayed a smile—a feeble effort. 'I always was a sucker for a sad story,' she tried to excuse her emotion.

But Mike was on his feet now, coming round the table to her, somehow managing to retain his grasp of her hand. 'Frankie,' his voice was husky, 'I proposed to you once—and you tore into me, treated it as a bad joke. But then, the other day, *you* mentioned marriage. As if you——'

'And this time *you* brushed it aside.' Frankie gulped. 'I can understand why, of course. You wouldn't want to risk a commitment like that again. But I'm the conventional type, Mike. I'm sorry, but a physical attraction isn't enough for me.'

Her words stopped him in his tracks.

'You mean. . .that's *all* you feel?' Now why did he sound so. . .so. . .agonised? 'Oh, Frankie.' And now he did drop her hand, turning away from her, leaning on the table as if he needed its support. 'Don't tell me I've made the same mistake twice.'

The smallest spark of hope suddenly began to flicker in Frankie's breast, so small that she hardly dared encourage it. And yet. . . She moved around him, so that she could see his face, put a tentative hand on his arm. 'Mike. . .do you mean. . .? No, you couldn't possibly——'

'Frankie,' he interrupted her, his dark eyes, their expression haunted, on her face, 'What I'm trying to say is, I'm in love with you. Why else for heaven's sake would I be so happy to be free at last of my enslavement to Liz?' And as she continued to stare at him, afraid to believe what she was hearing, 'I couldn't credit it myself at first—that I loved you, I mean. I knew I found you attractive. I always had, much against my will. Damn it, I found myself almost drooling over those photographs your aunt used to show me—the sheer sexuality of you. But I wasn't about to be beguiled by a beautiful face and body again. And as you know I wasn't too impressed at that time by what I saw as your wilful neglect of your aunt. When I *did* meet you I tried hard at first to convince myself that you were just a lovely empty shell. That the physical attraction I felt was understandable in view of my celibate life.'

'You. . .you mean you and Liz. . .you haven't. . .you didn't——'

'No, Frankie,' he said soberly, 'not for a very long time. We *were* divorced, you know, and although I was trying to persuade her to come back to me it didn't seem fair to cloud the issue. She had to come back to me because she loved me, not just because she wanted me. There is a difference.'

'Oh, I know!' Frankie breathed.

Mike put his hands on her shoulders and looked earnestly into her eyes. 'I know it's not long since you thought you were in love with Nigel. But I'm not flattering myself, am I? You don't find me *un*attractive?'

'Not in the least,' she told him and then, in case her remark might be considered ambiguous, 'I mean, I'm attracted to you very much. I——'

'But perhaps it's too soon for anything else? I've had two years to——'

'Mike.' Frankie didn't want to hear any more about Liz. Liz was his past now and she was beginning to believe that *she* might be his future, '*I* don't need two years.' Her expressive green eyes willed him to understand what she was saying.

'You mean——'

'I mean I love you.' And as he continued to stare at her as though he did not believe what he heard, 'For heaven's sake, Mike, kiss me.'

'Oh, Frankie!' His grasp tightened and an exquisite sense of anticipation built inside her, tensing her body with sensual hunger. 'You don't know how much I've been wanting this,' he muttered thickly. And as he lowered his head, enfolding her in his arms, her lips were already parted, welcoming his possession of them.

His kiss was fierce but no fiercer than her response, her body catching fire from his as his hands slid down her hips, pulling her against him, letting her feel his arousal.

His caresses became more and more sensual, his hand beneath her sweater capturing her breast, and he shivered as he felt its peaked response.

He lifted his head to stare hungrily into her face. 'Lord, but I want you, Frankie, I love you. Say you'll marry me. Say you love me again. That you'll never leave me. I want to hear you say it. Hear you say that life here in Lionswick will be enough for you—life with me. You're a different woman from the one in those photographs. But I think I'm still a little afraid that you'll change your mind, that your former existence will call you back again some day.'

'Never,' she said solemnly, her fingertips caressing the roughness of his cheek, her eyes begging him unashamedly to go on making love to her. He hadn't even shaved, she realised, before coming to her rescue. 'Even before I realised I was in love with you, even before I knew I had a chance with you, I'd made up my mind to stay. You were right, Mike, I never lost my affection for the countryside. But because of my loyalty to my mother I'd pushed it into the background, let other things, other people, smother it. With you,' she stood on tiptoe to brush her lips across his, 'I'm going to have the best of both worlds, my two loves in one.'

He rubbed his thumb over her mouth. 'Frankie,' he said huskily, 'if you go on looking at me like that, I won't be responsible for my actions. In fact, I think it might be better if we concerned ourselves with practicalities right now.' But he made no attempt to release her.

'I thought we'd taken care of practicalities for the moment,' Frankie murmured provocatively. 'I thought—in your words—we were going to take time out for ourselves.'

He pulled her so hard against him that she felt her ribcage would snap. With his face buried in her hair she could hardly hear what he was saying. 'Frankie, don't say things like that, unless you're prepared to take the consequences. I want you, I need you. But to quote *your* words, you're the conventional type. Doesn't that mean you'll want my ring on your finger before. . .?'

'No,' she managed to say against the barrier of his chest. And, demurely, as she was allowed a little more freedom of movement, 'I'm not *that* conventional.'

He scanned her face, his eyes darker than ever with the strength of his emotion, and a nerve ticked in his cheek. 'Does that mean what I think it means, that you'd let me make love to you—here—now?'

'There's only one thing stopping me from saying yes,' she told him wryly, 'the thought of that freezing cold bedroom.'

A smile twitched the corner of his mouth and lightened his eyes. 'Who needs bedrooms? Don't go away,' he bade her.

Puzzled, she watched as he strode from the room. But enlightenment was not long in coming. He returned, carrying the sofa cushions from the living-room, and set them down by the hearth where a healthy fire now burned. 'I don't suppose we'll be getting any visitors in this weather,' he said, 'but just in case. . .' He locked the back door and closed the curtains.

As he came towards her once more, Frankie swallowed nervously. She was shaking from head to foot. She wanted him so much but she was afraid now, not fear of her own disappointment but of his. She was still a virgin but Mike was an experienced man.

As soon as he took her in his arms he was aware of her condition. 'Not having second thoughts?' he asked.

She couldn't meet his eyes. 'No,' she whispered, head downbent. 'It's just. . .just that I haven't done this before.'

'Oh, my love!' He gathered her close. 'I promise you I won't rush or hurt you.'

'It's not that!' She had the courage to look at him now. 'I'm so afraid you'll be disappointed in me. That you'll——'

'Hush!' He closed her lips with his. 'Just relax. Everything is going to be just perfect.'

Slowly, oh, so slowly, he undressed her, allowing his fingers to caress each inch of flesh they exposed, making sensual hunger lick through her, making her moan low in her throat. As he found the front fastening of her bra and freed her soft curves, he bent his head, his tongue delicately tracing the dark aureoles, sending shudders of fierce pleasure through her.

He shed his own clothes more rapidly and Frankie watched him shyly. She had never seen a totally naked man before and the sight of his magnificent physique, the crisp dark body hair, was a revelation that filled her with coiling urgency.

He took her down with him on to the cushions, the glow of the fire warming, lighting their bodies with flickering flame.

His eyes worshipped her body, the high firm breasts, the narrow waist and flat stomach, the long slim legs. 'Beautiful,' he breathed, 'far more beautiful than any photograph.' His hands explored the curve of her hips, drew erotic designs over the quivering softness of her stomach, explored the soft indentation of her navel, moved lower to further intimacies, making her breath come in deep harsh gasps, teaching her things she had never known before. 'Touch *me*,' he demanded hoarsely. 'Touch me, Frankie. Love me.'

Frankie obeyed, letting her fingertips trace his taut body as he had outlined hers, awed by the intimacy of what she was doing.

Encouraged by him, she grew more daring, pressing tremulous kisses against his flesh, revelling in his primitive response. She wanted to be part of him, so completely a part that they would never be separated again.

'Dear lord, how I want you,' he breathed against her mouth. And she felt him shudder as she arched into him, too shy to tell him in words that she was ready for him.

The message of her body was received and answered as he moved above her, lifting and locking her against him. She felt a moment of panic as he entered her, but then it was gone, replaced by a burning urgency. Her arms locked about him, she responded to his ardent tutoring, losing herself in a storm of pleasure, and knowing that his enjoyment was as fierce as her own.

The storm passed but still they lay enfolded, side by side, wrapped in contentment.

'Frankie?' Mike's voice was questioning, anxious. 'Are you all right? I didn't mean it to happen so soon. But I couldn't hold back any longer. I didn't hurt you?'

She turned her head to look at him, eyes still glazed with love. 'I'm very much all right,' she told him softly. 'Oh, Mike, is it always like that?'

'For us,' he told her, 'please God, it always will be.'

Over his shoulder she stared dreamily into the fire, picturing in its flames their future together.

'Mike,' she asked suddenly, 'where shall we live? I mean, you have your house and I have this one.'

'Well,' he growled playfully, 'we certainly won't be living in separate houses. I must admit I hadn't given it much thought.' His voice deepened. 'In fact I hadn't thought much at all beyond loving you and wanting you.' He was silent for a moment, then, 'How would it be if we made *this* our home? It's larger for a start.' Huskily, 'Plenty of room for a family. You *would* like children?'

'Very much. But what about your house, the practice? Would you move that up here too?'

'No. It might be too much off the beaten track, especially in weather like today. I've been thinking for a while of taking on an assistant. The practice has grown a lot of late. As a lonely bachelor I didn't mind working all hours, being called out at night. 'But,' and his lips sought hers, 'all that is going to change.'

There was a long interval during which they confirmed very satisfactorily just how much both their lives were going to change.

'The assistant can use my house. And we'll concentrate on turning this one into a real home. Do you like that idea?'

'I like all your ideas,' Frankie murmured, her arms closing around him once more, 'but right now do you think we could concentrate on the best one of all?'

'What's that?' he teased.

Moving against him, she enlightened him, but without words.

HISTORICAL

CHRISTMAS

STORIES · 1991

Bring back heartwarming memories of Christmas past
with HISTORICAL CHRISTMAS STORIES 1991,
a collection of romantic stories
by three popular authors.
The perfect Christmas gift!

Don't miss these heartwarming stories,
available in November
wherever Harlequin books are sold:

CHRISTMAS YET TO COME
by Linda Trent
A SEASON OF JOY
by Caryn Cameron
FORTUNE'S GIFT
by DeLoras Scott

**Best Wishes and Season's Greetings
from Harlequin!**

XM-91

"INDULGE A LITTLE" SWEEPSTAKES

HERE'S HOW THE SWEEPSTAKES WORKS

NO PURCHASE NECESSARY

To enter each drawing, complete the appropriate Official Entry Form or a 3" by 5" index card by hand-printing your name, address and phone number and the trip destination that the entry is being submitted for (i.e., Walt Disney World Vacation Drawing, etc.) and mailing it to: Indulge '91 Subscribers-Only Sweepstakes, P.O. Box 1397, Buffalo, New York 14269-1397.

No responsibility is assumed for lost, late or misdirected mail. Entries must be sent separately with first class postage affixed, and be received by: 9/30/91 for the Walt Disney World Vacation Drawing, 10/31/91 for the Alaskan Cruise Drawing and 11/30/91 for the Hawaiian Vacation Drawing. Sweepstakes is open to residents of the U.S. and Canada, 21 years of age or older as of 11/7/91.

For complete rules, send a self-addressed, stamped (WA residents need not affix return postage) envelope to: Indulge '91 Subscribers-Only Sweepstakes Rules, P.O. Box 4005, Blair, NE 68009.

© 1991 HARLEQUIN ENTERPRISES LTD.   DIR-RL

"INDULGE A LITTLE" SWEEPSTAKES

HERE'S HOW THE SWEEPSTAKES WORKS

NO PURCHASE NECESSARY

To enter each drawing, complete the appropriate Official Entry Form or a 3" by 5" index card by hand-printing your name, address and phone number and the trip destination that the entry is being submitted for (i.e., Walt Disney World Vacation Drawing, etc.) and mailing it to: Indulge '91 Subscribers-Only Sweepstakes, P.O. Box 1397, Buffalo, New York 14269-1397.

No responsibility is assumed for lost, late or misdirected mail. Entries must be sent separately with first class postage affixed, and be received by: 9/30/91 for the Walt Disney World Vacation Drawing, 10/31/91 for the Alaskan Cruise Drawing and 11/30/91 for the Hawaiian Vacation Drawing. Sweepstakes is open to residents of the U.S. and Canada, 21 years of age or older as of 11/7/91.

For complete rules, send a self-addressed, stamped (WA residents need not affix return postage) envelope to: Indulge '91 Subscribers-Only Sweepstakes Rules, P.O. Box 4005, Blair, NE 68009.

© 1991 HARLEQUIN ENTERPRISES LTD.   DIR-RL

INDULGE A LITTLE—WIN A LOT!

Summer of '91 Subscribers-Only Sweepstakes

OFFICIAL ENTRY FORM

This entry must be received by: Oct. 31, 1991
This month's winner will be notified by: Nov. 7, 1991
Trip must be taken between: May 27, 1992—Sept. 9, 1992
(depending on sailing schedule)

YES, I want to win the Alaska Cruise vacation for two. I understand the prize includes round-trip airfare, one-week cruise including private cabin, all meals and pocket money as revealed on the "wallet" scratch-off card.

Name _____

Address_____ Apt. _____

City _____

State/Prov. _____ Zip/Postal Code _____

Daytime phone number _____
(Area Code)

Return entries with invoice in envelope provided. Each book in this shipment has two entry coupons—and the more coupons you enter, the better your chances of winning!

© 1991 HARLEQUIN ENTERPRISES LTD.   2N-CPS

INDULGE A LITTLE—WIN A LOT!

Summer of '91 Subscribers-Only Sweepstakes

OFFICIAL ENTRY FORM

This entry must be received by: Oct. 31, 1991
This month's winner will be notified by: Nov. 7, 1991
Trip must be taken between: May 27, 1992—Sept. 9, 1992
(depending on sailing schedule)

YES, I want to win the Alaska Cruise vacation for two. I understand the prize includes round-trip airfare, one-week cruise including private cabin, all meals and pocket money as revealed on the "wallet" scratch-off card.

Name _____

Address_____ Apt. _____

City _____

State/Prov. _____ Zip/Postal Code _____

Daytime phone number _____
(Area Code)

Return entries with invoice in envelope provided. Each book in this shipment has two entry coupons—and the more coupons you enter, the better your chances of winning!

© 1991 HARLEQUIN ENTERPRISES LTD.   2N-CPS